TASK
s/o
8.99

BEYOND THE HORIZON

Kate Christian was shocked and angry when she learnt that her father had been dismissed from his job as head gardener at The Grange by the new owner, Sir Peter Grenville. In the depressed thirties, work was scarce, and there wasn't much call for gardeners on the Isle of Man, so Kate decides to go and confront Sir Peter. However, it is his son, Roger, who agrees to see her. But how can Kate remain calm when she finds him so attractive?

SHIRLEY ALLEN

BEYOND THE HORIZON

Complete and Unabridged

LINFORD
Leicester

First published in Great Britain in 2003

First Linford Edition
published 2004

British Library CIP Data

Allen, Shirley
    Beyond the horizon.—Large print ed.—
    Linford romance library
    1. Isle of Man—Social life and customs
    —Fiction 2. Love stories
    3. Large type books
    I. Title
    823.9′2 [F]

    ISBN 1–84395–619–5

Published by
F. A. Thorpe (Publishing)
Anstey, Leicestershire

Set by Words & Graphics Ltd.
Anstey, Leicestershire
Printed and bound in Great Britain by
T. J. International Ltd., Padstow, Cornwall

This book is printed on acid-free paper

1

'Mum, I'm home,' Kate Christian called as she opened the door of the small, terraced house where she lived with her parents and two younger sisters. She had an elder brother, John, but he was in the Navy and was seldom home. She went into the living-room and put her bag of books and papers down on the old, battered settee.

'Hello, love. How did your day go?'

Margaret Christian was barely forty, and had been a beauty in her youth. Now, however, her hair was liberally streaked with grey. Kate, a very pretty girl of nineteen, with bobbed blonde hair, smiled at her mother.

'Very well! Mrs Rogers said that I'm doing really well with my shorthand and . . .'

She broke off, her face suddenly bewildered, as she saw that her father was sitting in his armchair by the fire.

'Dad! What are you doing here?'

'Hush now, Kate,' her mother replied wearily.

Walter Christian put his mug of tea down on the worn table.

'No, love, don't tell her to be quiet. She'll have to know sooner or later, so it might as well be now. Kate, love, there's a new owner at The Grange, a fellow from Kent, he is, and he's brought his own gardener with him.'

'But, Dad, you've been working for Mr Quilliam for years. He thought the world of you!'

Her father gave a tired smile.

'Yes, Kate, Thomas Quilliam was a fine employer, but didn't you hear what I said? He's gone. Sold the place to Sir Peter Grenville.'

'Gone! But you were there on Saturday morning, and it's only Monday now. He can't have just up and gone that quickly!'

'But he has, pet, and I can tell you for why. The mine wasn't doing well, he was in debt and he had to sell, and sell quickly. I'd known for a while that The Grange was up for sale. I just hadn't expected things to happen so fast.'

Kate turned to her mother.

'Did you know about this?' she asked, shock in her voice.

Walter Christian answered for his wife.

'No, because I saw no reason to tell her. I didn't want to upset your mother about something which I thought wouldn't happen for a while yet.'

He sighed, and Kate realised, with a pang, that he looked like an old man.

'Anyway, I didn't think there was any need to. I thought that the new owner would be keeping on the existing staff.'

'But, Dad, even if he has brought a gardener with him, you were head gardener to Mr Quilliam. Ned and Bill were working under you!'

'They'll be staying. I said that this fellow, this Sir Peter, brought his gardener with him, and he has, his head gardener.'

'Then you're out of a job, just like that?' Kate said, her voice incredulous.

'Yes, just like that. It's the way of the aristocracy, so it seems. I was dismissed on the spot, and after having worked at The Grange for nigh on twenty five years! Not that he saw me off without a penny, so to speak. I got thirty shillings, a week's wages in lieu of notice.'

'Oh, Dad, what a terrible thing to happen!'

In the depressed Thirties, work was scarce, and the Isle of Man was certainly not a prosperous place, peopled as it was with farmers and fishermen. Oh, the landladies of the numerous boarding houses thronged on Douglas promenade did well enough, but even their livelihoods looked to be increasingly in jeopardy with Adolf Hitler making threatening noises in far away Germany. But that was what it was — far away.

But her father was a very good gardener, he truly was, and, as he had said, he'd worked for Mr Quilliam for twenty-five years. Surely he wouldn't have trouble in obtaining another position. Then she bit her lip. Was there much call for gardeners on an island that wasn't renowned for its wealth? There were a few wealthy families, and, of course, there was the Lieutenant Governor, but he likely had his staff brought in from the mainland.

'I've been down to the Labour Exchange,' her father said. 'They've taken my name, but they've no openings on their books for gardeners at the moment. They said that there may be openings for farm work though, so that would be better than nowt.'

'Farm work!'

Kate couldn't quite disguise the note of horror in her voice.

'But, Dad, you'd be a labourer, and you wouldn't take kindly to that after having virtually been your own boss!'

'Beggars can't be choosers, Kate. I'll be lucky to get taken on for that, seeing as there's plenty of young fellows around.'

'But, Dad, you're not old!'

'I'm forty-five, and that's old enough when it comes to looking for work!'

A sob escaped Margaret Christian's lips, and she mumbled, 'I need to be on my own!'

As she fled from the room, Walter shook his head.

'I shouldn't have said as much. Your mother has a nervous temperament.'

'It's my fault, Dad. I shouldn't have pressed you,' Kate replied gently. 'Don't fret, something will turn up. I'd better go and see how Mum is.'

She hurried out of the room and up the stairs after her mother.

Margaret Christian was lying on her bed, crying.

'Oh, Mum, don't take on so!'

Kate threw herself down beside her mother and put her arms around the trembling woman.

'It's not the end of the world, you know. Dad has years of experience behind him. He'll have a job in next to no time, just you wait and see!'

Margaret pushed herself up against the pillows.

'You don't understand it yet, do you?'

Her voice was hoarse with the sobs she was desperately trying to stifle.

'Well, of course I do!' Kate protested. 'Dad has been paid off, and it's a terrible shame, totally unjust, but as I said, he . . . '

Margaret, her face red and blotchy, smiled wanly.

'It's not just the job, Kate. It's the house! The house goes with the job, and, quite obviously, this Sir Peter is a hard-hearted wretch! He wants our house for his fellow, this gardener that he's brought over here with him. And do you know what?'

Kate didn't reply. She was horrified to realise that she hadn't even thought of the fact that the house went with the job.

'He's given your father a week, just one miserly week to find somewhere else to live!' her mother went on.

7

Kate swallowed. It certainly wasn't much time, but they'd find somewhere else. They'd have to! After all, Dad could claim National Assistance, and they had their savings, so they wouldn't be absolutely destitute. Then she smiled grimly. They didn't have much savings. For all that Mr Quilliam had been a good employer, wages just weren't very high, and the house had served as part of her father's pay anyway.

She stood up, having suddenly arrived at a decision.

'I'll find a job.'

'No,' Margaret protested vehemently.

'But, Mum, it's the most sensible thing to do. I can easily get something in one of the fish factories. The work is hard, but they do pay very well.'

Margaret's face was grimly determined.

'You will not! I worked there myself before I married your father and I know just how awful it is to be standing on a cold concrete floor for ten hours a day gutting slimy, smelly fish! No, my girl, you're going to finish your course and get a good job!'

'But, Mum, I don't mind! Meg and Jessie are only eight and six. They've got to go to school, but I've finished my education. The shorthand and typing course was a luxury, and not for the likes of us!'

Kate could tell that her mother was about to protest further, so she hurried on.

'Besides, it isn't cheap training to be a secretary. There won't be the money for it!'

Margaret's mouth wobbled and she looked as if she might burst into tears again. Kate quickly put her arm back around her mother's shoulders.

'Kate, love, it's early days yet. Let's just wait and see how things go. Why, if the worst comes to the worse, we can always split up. I know Elsie and Fred would take me and the girls. They haven't a lot of room, but they'd squeeze us in somewhere, and you could perhaps stay with one of your friends at the secretarial school. As for your father, well, he could probably find a live-in job on one of the farms.'

Kate was horrified.

'But, Mum, you couldn't possibly do something like that! Our family has always been together and that's the way I intend it to remain! Anyway, you know full well that Uncle Fred and Auntie Elsie haven't got any room. They've only got a two-up-and-two-down, and four children! And as for my friends at the school, well . . . '

She broke off. How could she tell her already-distressed mother that she had no friends at Clareville Secretarial College for Young Ladies, that the other girls, from middle-class backgrounds, looked down on her because she lived in one of the poorer parts of the town?

'I didn't say it would come to that. I don't think it will for a moment.'

Margaret forced a cheerfulness which she certainly wasn't feeling in her voice.

'I only meant if the worst came to the worst, but it won't, love. As you said, your father can claim National Assistance, thank goodness, and although it's not much, it's enough to pay the rent on another place.'

That it wouldn't be enough to pay rent and feed them, Margaret didn't mention, although both women were acutely aware of the fact.

'It's a pity our John doesn't see fit to send money home more often!' Kate replied bitterly. 'But he was always a selfish one, and with him away at sea, well, it's hard to get in touch with him!'

Her only son was Margaret Christian's favourite child, probably because he was the only boy. She wasn't going to stand by and hear him criticised, even if in her heart of hearts she knew that her eldest daughter was right.

'You can't expect a lad of twenty to be always thinking of his family,' she replied. 'Besides, he doesn't earn much and needs the money for himself.'

'That he does not! He's fed and clothed by the Navy. He doesn't give a jot about anyone else, and never has done!'

'Now, Kate, I'll not be having you criticising your brother like that! The food is poor in the Navy. The lad's said so in his letters. He needs his money to get himself stuff he can eat.'

'A likely story!' Kate snorted derisively.

'It's true. That's what he always says in his letters.'

'When he gets around to actually writing one! He's been in the Navy since he was seventeen, and how many times have you heard from him, three, isn't it?'

Margaret's face crumpled, and Kate was afraid that her mother was going to cry again.

'Oh, Mum, I'm sorry, I shouldn't have said that! I realise that young men aren't good letter writers. John was never fond of putting pen to paper.'

'He's a good lad,' Margaret said stubbornly. 'If he knew about this, he'd be the first one to help, you know he would, but as you said, we can't get in touch with him very easily.'

'You could write and tell him, or I can, but it'll take a while to reach him.'

Margaret, however, seemed cheered by this remark.

'I'll fetch my paper and write to him straightaway,' she said.

Kate forced a smile to her lips.

'Yes, do that, Mum. I'm sure he'll want to know, and that he'll help.'

God forgive me for telling lies, she thought, as she left her mother sitting writing to her beloved, and singularly unworthy, son.

It was a fraught, tension-filled week. Walter spent most of his time either at the Labour Exchange, or looking for a house he could rent cheaply for his family. He had some luck, but not a lot. As he had predicted, most of the local farmers considered him too old to take on as a hired hand, but on the fifth day of his search, Dan Kelly agreed to take him on. Initially it would be temporary, but if Walter proved to be satisfactory, the farmer told him that he would probably keep him on permanently. The trouble was that the work was poorly paid, the hours long, and he was expected to live in, something which he was most unhappy about.

Margaret didn't like the idea any better than her husband, but what choice did they have? At least he would be earning more than the pittance which the Labour Exchange handed out, and, anyway, if one refused to take up an offer of employment the dole money was usually stopped.

'I'll go to Elsie's with the girls.'

Margaret, having spoken to her sister, had been assured that she would never see Margaret stuck. Walter wasn't too happy about the idea, however.

'What about Kate? Where's she going to go?'

Kate, coming into the room, forced a cheerfulness into her voice which she certainly didn't feel.

'Oh, I'll be all right. Don't worry about me at all! Cathy Cregeen has said that I can come and stay with her and her family for as long as I like.'

Margaret frowned.

'Cathy Cregeen? Who's she, love?'

'Oh, just a girl I'm friendly with. Her father's a banker.'

Both Margaret and Walter looked suitably impressed, as Kate had known they would.

'A banker? Well, we are moving in exalted circles, aren't we, little Katie?'

This was the name he had called her when she was a little girl. It made Kate feel as if she wanted to burst into tears. Oh, if only there was a Cathy Cregeen, and if only she was really going to stay with her! But Kate had made up her mind, and had spoken to Mrs Rogers. Tears threatened in Kate's eyes as she remembered how kind the principal of Clareville Secretarial School had been.

'But, Kate, you can't up and leave in the middle of your course! Why, you're my very best student, in fact, I think you're easily one of the most gifted girls whom I've ever taught!'

Kate had smiled sadly.

'Thank you for saying so, Mrs Rogers, but I can't stay on, not with my family in the predicament that they're in. They just won't be able to keep supporting me.'

'My dear, I have a suggestion to put to you.'

Eleanor Rogers had looked at Kate over her horn-rimmed spectacles.

'If you are agreeable, I will continue to let you stay on here free of charge.'

But Kate had shaken her head.

'That's very, very kind of you, Mrs Rogers, but I couldn't take charity. My parents wouldn't allow it, and anyway, I have to find somewhere to stay, so I think that my best bet is to look for a live-in position.'

'I may be able to help you there,' the principal had said, 'and in the mean-time, my dear, you can stay with my sister, Mrs Jackson.'

As Kate opened her mouth to protest, Eleanor Rogers held up a hand.

'No, child, it most definitely won't be

charity! My sister is a disabled lady, and, I have to confess, something of a tyrant. She is expecting a new girl to come from England in a couple of weeks' time, but for now, I know that she will certainly be glad of you. I don't know how happy you'll be with Amelia, but at least you'll have a roof over your head until we can come up with something more suitable, and I will see that she allows you a half-day off a week, as well as Sunday afternoon, so that you can come here and continue with your studies, albeit in a small way.'

'Ma'am, that's extremely kind of you,' Kate had replied, then a thought had struck her. 'But what shall I say to my parents? Dad will still try to struggle to pay my fees, for they both insist that I finish my education.'

'Tell them that I will hold over payment of fees for the next month, and then we'll review the situation. Do you think that their pride will allow them to agree to that, my dear?'

Kate had almost hugged Mrs Rogers.

17

'Yes,' she had said, eyes distinctly moist now. 'I'm sure that will suit them very well.'

Although Walter had made a token protest, that was all it had been. Actually, he had been relieved when Kate told him of Mrs Rogers' offer to leave the fees over for a month to give the family a chance to find their feet.

'And she only said that she'd review the situation after that, Dad,' Kate said. 'I really feel that she'd agree to longer. She's a very kind lady and . . . '

'And she knows that you're a very fine pupil!' Margaret said. 'You could do very well in life, Kate, and I want you to have all the chances that I didn't have. I was ambitious as a girl, you know. Wanted to be an actress, I did. I even starred at the Gaiety Theatre in Oscar Wilde's Lady Windermere's Fan. I played the lady herself. My mother thought that I was mad, so she did! But then, she had ten kids to contend with, so I suppose the poor woman had enough to think about without having a budding actress in the family!'

'Your mam did very well, love. I was very fond of the old girl,' Walter said, a trifle wistfully, as his mind went back into the past. 'Sometimes I think it's a pity that they all left the island apart from Elsie and Flo. And why Flo went into St Catherine's to be a nun, I'll never know!'

'My mam was Irish, Walter, and our Florence, well, she was always different from the others. She wanted peace and quiet.'

Walter laughed.

'Yes, I suppose that was it, love. She certainly wouldn't have got much of that at home! But at least yours was a happy house. My pa scarpered off with some Liverpool woman when Dick and I were only kids! She had a hard time, did my ma. She had to take in washing and ironing to keep a roof over our heads and even then, we never had enough to eat. Not that I'm complaining, mind. I just don't want that kind of things for our kids.'

'It won't be like that, Dad,' Kate said, soothingly.

She knew her father wasn't happy about going to work for Dan Kelly, who was well known to be stingy, for all that his farm was quite a prosperous one. Worse still, Walter didn't want to be separated from his family.

'It won't be for long,' Margaret said soothingly. 'I don't want to be a burden on our Elsie. Not that I won't help her with the house and such, I will, glad to have something to do, to take my mind off things, so to speak.'

'We should be thankful,' Kate said, 'because at least we've all got somewhere to go, even if it isn't what we'd have from choice.'

As soon as she'd said it, Kate wished she could bite the words back. Her father was immediately anxious.

'What do you mean, love? I thought you'd be happy with this friend of yours, the banker's daughter, and Mrs Rogers being so kind to you and all.'

'Oh, I am!' Kate instantly assured

20

him. 'It's just the thought of the family being parted that I don't like. We've never been separated like this.'

Walter reached for his pipe.

'Don't fret, love. I certainly don't intend working for old man Kelly for the rest of my life, and that's a fact! But you'll be getting your education, and you'll be with your friend.'

He smiled at his eldest daughter, his favourite child, his little Katie.

Kate walked over to her father and planted a kiss on his head.

'Dad,' she said, 'you've been wonderful, the best father anyone could ever wish for!'

His cheeks coloured. He wasn't a man used to flattery.

'Ah, away with you, lass! You're coming over all sentimental now, and I can't handle it.'

He turned to his wife.

'Mags, would you mind if I went down to the Manxman for a pint? You know I'm not a drinking man, but this past week has been hard. I feel I could do with meeting up with some of my old mates.'

Margaret smiled wistfully. She had a very good husband, and she would miss him dreadfully, despite being with her own daughter, Elsie, Fred and their brood.

'Go and have a couple, lad, it'll do you good.'

'Will you come with me?' he asked suddenly. 'There's a snug, so you won't be embarrassed.'

Margaret's hesitation was only momentary. He'd said that he wanted to meet up with his mates, but clearly he wanted her company. She wasn't a drinker, but she supposed she could have a port and lemon.

Kate felt it was time to leave her parents alone.

'Enjoy yourselves,' she said, knowing that her mother would go. 'I'll see how the girls are doing with their home-work. And there's no need to hurry back, neither, for I'll see to their suppers and get them off to bed.'

Margaret, ever emotional, looked at her daughter with moist eyes.

'Thank you, Kate, you're a treasure.'

She wasn't, Kate thought, as she went upstairs to the tiny room which her sisters shared. No, rather, she was a liar, for she hadn't exactly told her parents the truth. Still, it was with good intentions, she consoled herself, as she entered the girls' room and tried to inject some enthusiasm for homework into two singularly unwilling pupils.

It was on the next morning, Saturday, and therefore a free day for Kate, that she made a decision. It certainly wasn't something which she had planned to do, and yet, for some reason, not really known to herself, she found herself making her way to The Grange, an imposing eighteenth-century mansion on Douglas Head, looking over the bay.

Kate, you're an idiot, she chided herself, as she trudged up the very steep hill which led to The Grange. What on earth are you going to say to this fellow, this Sir Peter? He's going to think that you're a complete fool! Still she walked on, opening the gate, and making her way down the tree-lined drive. She had to say something to the arrogant fellow. She owed it to her father.

Holding her breath, she lifted the elaborate door knocker, a gargoyle, she saw with a half-nervous, half-wry smile — probably appropriate!

'Yes?' a snooty-faced maid, dressed in black, asked, as she opened the heavy, oaken door.

'I've come to see Sir Peter. Is he in?' Kate asked, without preamble, although her hands were clammy.

'Are you expected?' the maidservant asked, in a voice which immediately told Kate that the girl knew full well that she wasn't.

'Well, no,' she admitted ruefully. 'But I do want to see him. I have to!'

The servant raised her eyebrows.

'Sir Peter is at home,' she admitted, 'but I'm not at all sure that he will wish to see you! Who are you anyway, and what do you want?'

'My name is Katherine Christian, as to my business that's between him and me, not you and me!'

The pert nose wrinkled.

'Are you looking for a job? Because if so, you go to the tradesmen's entrance at the side of the house, and you ask to see Mrs Scott, the housekeeper.'

'I'm not looking for a job,' Kate replied, and then she hesitated.

On second thoughts, why not? After all, life with Mrs Rogers' invalid sister didn't sound exactly fun, and, more important, it was only temporary.

'Yes, I had thought to seek a position here,' Kate said. 'But do I really have to go to the tradesmen's entrance? Isn't that rather archaic?'

The girl opened her mouth. This was a queer one, right enough.

'You said your name is Katherine Christian, didn't you?'

Kate nodded, and the maid sighed.

'All right, if you'll just wait here, I'll go and see if Sir Peter is prepared to see you, or if he would prefer you to see Mrs Scott.'

Kate smiled. She'd won! Well, it was only the first round, of course, but at least she was going to get a foothold inside The Grange.

2

The maid, Violet, nervously relayed to Sir Peter that he had a visitor, someone called Katherine Christian.

Sir Peter looked a trifle vague, after all, he had had rather a lot to contend with of late. He wondered why he had decided to move to the Isle of Man. Why the devil had he thought it sensible to come to such a backwoods? But life in London had become boring and repetitive. His wife, Lady Alicia, seemed to think that it was obligatory to party every night, and then there was the ever-increasing prospect of war with Nazi Germany. London certainly wouldn't be the best place to live if such an occurrence did come about, and Sir Peter was becoming more and more certain that it would.

Then there was his first-born, his son and heir, and here, Sir Peter groaned audibly, as he looked at his eldest son. Oh, Roger was a handsome enough chap, very handsome, if his father was going to be fair to him, but he was still a bitter disappointment to his father. His mother, Lady Alicia, seemed to dote on him. The young fellow was a very good-looking chap, but after having said that, he didn't have a lot else going for him. He was a dreamer, a thinker, an artist.

Sir Peter shuddered. Art was all very well in its place, but Roger had carried it too far. He'd spent three years in an attic flat in Paris, and he had achieved results. He had had three exhibitions of his paintings, two in Paris and one in London. Some fool had even referred to him as the new Van Gogh, but who would want a crackpot like Vincent Van Gogh for a son?

Sir Peter suddenly remembered that the maid was waiting to see if he would receive his unexpected visitor.

'What does the woman want

anyway?' he asked at last.

'I don't know, sir. She wouldn't tell me. Said as good as it was none of my business and that she would only speak to you. Mind, then she relented a bit and I did get the idea that she was thinking of asking if there were any jobs going here.'

Roger, who had been sitting quietly listening to the conversation with an increasing spark of interest, said, 'You don't need to bother your head about all this, Father. I know that you've got quite enough to occupy yourself with just now. Suppose I see her. She hasn't met you, after all, so she won't know that I'm not you, will she?'

Sir Peter sighed.

'Roger, what are you up to now?'

His voice was weary. The past few weeks had been very tiresome.

'Why do you want to speak to some woman whom we neither know, nor, I should imagine, wish to know?'

'Because the situation intrigues me. There must be a reason for it. Didn't you say that you'd sacked Mr Quilliam's head gardener?'

'Yes, but what the devil has that got to do with it?'

'I'm not sure yet, but if my memory serves me correctly, I thought you said that the man's name was Christian.'

'It could have been,' Sir Peter admitted. 'Oh, go and do what you want! You will anyway, so there's little point in me trying to stop you!'

Roger Grenville, tall, fair and handsome, six foot one, and twenty-three years of age, smiled at his father.

'Thank you, Father. This should be a very interesting experience!'

'Oh, just go!' Sir Peter said, shaking his head.

Kate was standing just inside the door where the maid had left her, when a strikingly good-looking young man appeared. Kate gasped. Surely this couldn't be Sir Peter Grenville. Surely he wasn't old enough. Certainly he wasn't a bit like she had pictured the new owner of The Grange. She knew that she was standing looking at him with her mouth slightly agape, but she just couldn't help it.

The newcomer laughed at her expression quite openly, and Kate felt ready colour flare into her cheeks. How dare he laugh at her!

'I don't know why you should find it amusing, sir,' she said stiffly, 'or perhaps sacking innocent people is sport for the gentry.'

He immediately became serious.

'Forgive me, Miss Christian, I wasn't laughing at the fact that my . . . that I had to most regretfully inform your father that his services were no longer required owing to the fact that I have my own head gardener. I was laughing at your expression. You looked amazed when you saw me. May I ask why that should be?'

He had a very nice speaking voice, she had to admit.

'I didn't expect you to be so young,' she replied truthfully — nor as good-looking, she could have added,

31

but sensibly refrained from doing so.

'Ah, no, well, I think that I have been lucky in the fact that the years have treated me kindly,' he replied, smiling. 'But let's not talk standing out here. Would you come to my study, please? We can talk more comfortably there.'

And he started along the hall, Kate following him. Her mind was in something of a turmoil, for he looked and seemed a pleasant young man. Yet how could he be, she asked herself, when he had treated her poor father so harshly?

'This is my study,' Roger said, opening a heavy, oak door and indicating that Kate should go into the room.

'Please, take a seat, wherever you like. I don't hold with too much formality, and then you can tell me what I can do for you, and I will do my best to oblige.'

Kate sat down gingerly on the very edge of a beautifully-upholstered red velvet chair. He hid a smile. She wasn't as at ease as she was trying to make out. Well, he couldn't blame her for that. It must have been quite daunting for her coming to The Grange, but he found himself admiring her for having the spirit to do so.

'May I offer you some refreshment?' he asked politely. 'Coffee, or perhaps you would prefer a glass of wine.'

'In the morning!'

Kate looked, and sounded, shocked.

'No, perhaps not,' he agreed, still the essence of good manners. 'But I'm sure that coffee will not go amiss, unless you would rather have tea.'

'Really, there's no need . . . ' she began, feeling confused by his solicitous attitude and not understanding it at all.

'Nonsense!' he said, but the word was spoken kindly, as he reached over and rang a bell, which, Kate gathered, would summon one of the servants.

'Now, I understand from Violet, the maid who let you in, that you might be looking for employment.'

'I was thinking along those lines, yes,' Kate replied, her head coming up and her blue eyes looking into his in defiance. 'After all, since you put my father out of a job, and with no notice to speak of, things haven't been . . . '

She broke off as there was a tap at the door, and on Roger saying, 'Come in,' the door opened to admit an older woman, dressed almost entirely in black.

'Oh, Mrs Quayle, it was good of you to answer. I was expecting one of the young maids.'

'They're all busy, sir, so I thought I'd come myself.'

'Well, if you would be kind enough to fetch a pot of coffee and some cakes, I would be most grateful.'

'Very good, sir,' the woman replied, even bobbing a somewhat archaic curtsey, then, throwing a curious look in Kate's direction, she hurried off to do the master's bidding.

'Are you suffering financial hardship, Katherine?' he asked, and she was surprised to see that there was genuine concern in his eyes, but then he had the grace to look a bit embarrassed. 'Sorry, I shouldn't have called you Katherine without first asking your permission. Forgive me, Miss Christian.'

'Kate,' she said. 'I'm known as Kate.'

He smiled.

'Well, thank you for allowing me to address you by your Christian name.'

She laughed, and there was bitterness in the sound.

'But why shouldn't you, sir? You're gentry, whilst I'm one of the poor, island natives. I believe some of you people refer to us as such.'

He looked ashamed.

'I haven't been here long enough to know how some people act, Kate, but I assure you that I would never refer to the local people as natives. To my mind, I'm the incomer to your country, and I will certainly try not to be an encumbrance, or to tread on anyone's toes.'

Kate shook her head in an effort to clear it. Sir Peter Grenville sounded nice. Yet how could he be, when he had so cursorily dismissed her father? No, he was the enemy, he must be, and she mustn't allow herself to weaken towards him, mustn't allow herself to see him as a kind and handsome young gentleman. No, she would do much better to go back to her previous mental picture of Sir Peter, a devil with two horns!

'But you've already trodden on someone's toes, haven't you, Sir Peter? My father's!'

He sighed at the bitterness in Kate's voice.

'I'm sorry about your father, Kate, I truly am.'

Oh, goodness! Had this charade of his been one of his best ideas? He was starting to find it difficult pretending to be his father, especially with those so earnest, but at the moment distinctly fiery pale blue eyes holding his with frightening intensity.

He was glad when Mrs Quayle arrived carrying a tray with a silver coffee pot, milk, two delicate china cups and saucers, and a tempting array of cakes and sandwiches. It was highly unlikely that they would eat them, of course. Roger knew that his appetite had left him completely, but still, he had felt it necessary to make the gesture, to treat Kate Christian as a lady. That was what she looked, for all that her clothes weren't of the best quality or the latest mode, and she was a strikingly attractive young woman, he admitted to himself, with a wry smile, so perhaps that was colouring his judgment, too.

'Shall I pour?' Mrs Quayle asked.

Roger shook his head. He wanted the woman out of the room as quickly as possible. After all, she knew who he was, so the longer she stayed, the more likelihood there was of her giving him away.

'I'll do it,' he said.

'As you wish, sir.'

She shuffled out of the room. Her bunions were troubling her a lot today, but if they hadn't been, she would have been a lot more curious as to why Roger Grenville was entertaining Katherine Christian in his study, for she had now remembered who the young woman was.

Roger poured Kate a cup of coffee and handed it to her. Then he offered her a cake or a sandwich, which she refused. Oh, they looked tempting enough, but she wasn't going to take the enemy's food, leastways, not unless she was to be employed by this man, and had earned it.

'Are you sure?' he asked politely. 'They'll probably only go to waste.'

Kate scowled. To waste such fine fare was criminal. The girls would have loved those fancy little cakes, but she wasn't going to say that to him.

'Well, eat it yourself then, or give it to the birds. They'll be glad enough of it!' she said instead.

'You've an acid tongue, Kate,' he replied, but he looked amused.

'Well, you can hardly expect me to be thrilled with you for putting my father out of work after twenty-five years working here for Mr Quilliam, now, can you?'

'No,' he said. 'To be honest, I think it's a perfectly shocking thing to do and I . . . '

He had been about to say that he didn't agree with it at all. He bit his tongue, and winced. Would he never remember that he was supposed to be his father? As it was, he fancied that Kate was looking at him curiously.

'I can't understand you, sir,' she admitted. 'You seem to be, well, quite human and I had visualised you very differently. Oh, I don't know. You don't look the kind of employer to sack a man just like that, and yet that's what you've done. I can't make head nor tail of it!'

'I felt that my first loyalty must be to the chap who was working for me back in England. He's been with me a long time, and he's a very good gardener.'

'So is my father, and he was with Mr Quilliam twenty-five years!' Kate retorted.

'Yes, so I understand. But Danny

Roberts has been with the family for . . . '

Dash! How long had the man worked for his father? Roger hadn't a clue.

'Oh, a good number of years, I forget exactly,' he stammered.

'Well, you would, wouldn't you? You probably don't take enough interest in the mere servants. Probably you leave such matters to an underling.'

Then she remembered that she had thought to try and get a job at The Grange and had the grace to look slightly abashed. The way she was carrying on, he would think her a very ignorant young woman, and would likely show her the door, given much more provocation.

'I'm sorry,' Kate said, but with ill grace. 'I shouldn't have said that.'

He smiled, a most attractive smile, Kate thought, albeit reluctantly. He had very white teeth. But then, his skin was tanned. No doubt he spent time in somewhere like the South of France.

'There's no need to apologise to me,'

he said, sounding sincere. 'I can understand that you must be feeling bitter. Has your father found another position?'

'Yes,' she admitted, 'but it's not much, not what he's been used to. He's going to be a farm labourer, and he'll have to live in, which is a crying shame, seeing as how it's going to break up the family.'

Roger was shocked.

'But surely his wife, your mother, surely she'll be going with him?'

Kate shook her head, a strand of blonde hair, which she had loosely bound into a chignon, falling across her face. She brushed it out of her eyes with impatient fingers.

'No, that's not the way of things. At his age, my father was lucky to get anything at all. Most of the farm-labouring jobs are taken by the young lads without families, so I suppose it was good of Dan Kelly, the farmer, to take him on. Mind, he'll make him earn his keep. Old man Kelly isn't known for his generosity.'

Roger was appalled.

'But what is your mother going to do?'

'She's going to Elsie, her sister, with the two girls, my two younger sisters. They're only bairns, really. Meg's eight and Jessie's six. They'll be all right there, though,' she added, her chin coming up defiantly. 'Auntie Elsie and Uncle Fred may have their own brood of four, and only a two-up, two-down, but they're family, and family look after their own!'

No wonder she was bitter, Roger thought, turning his head slightly away from her, so that she wouldn't see the troubled look in his eyes. His father was a very selfish man, and Roger would have something to say to him, not that he was likely to listen, of course. Roger knew that he was a disappointment to his father, who didn't approve of his interest in art. Mother wasn't much better, but he might be able to prevail upon her to do something. He smiled grimly. That was if she could bear to tear herself away from London, and the endless circle of parties and mindless frivolities.

He turned back, and Kate was looking at him expectantly, waiting for him to answer.

'I'm sorry for your family,' he admitted. 'I'm not really used to island life yet. I've been here on several visits, of course, but visiting and living somewhere are two entirely different things.'

Sorry for them! He had the nerve to say that he was sorry for her family when he, and no-one else, had caused their present predicament! Seeing the luxury of The Grange, his exquisite clothes, Kate's heart hardened towards him once again.

'It's very kind of you to say so, sir, I'm sure,' she said now, sarcasm evident in her voice. 'Wait until I tell them. I'm sure that they'll be very touched and comforted.'

If she did tell them — well, maybe

sometime, but the pretence of her staying with her school friend, Cathy, needed to be maintained for the foreseeable future. He wasn't to know that, though.

Roger sighed. Why the devil had he thought it fun to get involved? It was turning out to be anything but fun.

'Why did you come here?' he asked, getting to the point. 'Violet seemed to think that you could be interested in seeing if there was a position here available for you. Have you experience of domestic work?'

'No,' she said bluntly. 'I've been studying at the Clareville Secretarial College and I was intending to seek work for the government as a stenographer. But even before this, my parents were having difficulty paying my fees.'

She put a hand to her head, where a dull headache was beginning to make its presence felt. Oh, why was she telling him all this? There was no way in which he could possibly be the slightest bit interested!

'Yes, I do need a job,' she said, and, even to her own ears, her voice suddenly sounded tired, defeated, even.

'Then I will see what can be arranged,' he said, 'but your education is so important. Is there no way you can continue with it?'

'Mrs Rogers, she's the headmistress, has been very kind. She's agreed to let me come to the school on a weekday afternoon so that I can continue in a small way. She isn't going to charge for that.'

'She sounds like an admirable lady, but perhaps it may be possible to do something a little better than that. I take it that you wish to live in, seeing as how your aunt already seems to be rather overburdened.

'Yes, I need a live-in position,' Kate replied truthfully.

Mrs Rogers' sister sounded a virago, and in any event, the work there was of a very temporary nature. Kate definitely needed a roof over her head.

'It's possible that there will be

secretarial work required here. It may be only of a part-time nature, but if you were to have food and board, even if your wage wasn't particularly high, you would have more time to study, and perhaps to go to your Mrs Rogers.'

Kate's eyes were suddenly shining.

'Sir, that would be wonderful!' she exclaimed.

'Well, I cannot promise anything yet, you understand,' he replied, hating himself when he saw the light die in her eyes. 'But I will certainly do my best. Can you come here tomorrow round the same time?'

It was funny, it was almost as if he had to consult someone, Kate thought. Perhaps his wife, yes, that was probably it. The thought saddened her a little, and yet she didn't really know why.

'I'll come tomorrow,' she said, getting to her feet. 'Thank you for the coffee, and for giving me hope. I can see my way out. Goodbye for now.'

'Nonsense! I'll see you to the door,'

he said firmly, and he escorted her off the premises.

He stood at the door watching her walk down the long driveway. She didn't look back once. Frowning to himself, he went back into the house and closed the heavy door behind him. She was a spirited miss was Kate Christian, and he had to admit that she interested him, interested him quite a lot. He smiled as he wondered what her dear father would think of that.

3

Roger sought out his father after Kate's departure. He would have preferred to have spoken to his mother, Lady Alicia, but she was still in London, and not expected on the island for another few days yet.

'Well, what is it?' Sir Peter asked irritably.

He was in his study poring over paperwork. The paperwork was to do with opening a munitions' factory on the island, convinced as he was that there would be a war with Germany.

He frowned, however. The Manx government, after having made co-operative noises when he had sounded them out during one of his frequent visits to the island, was now being awkward. They weren't convinced that the situation in Germany would lead to war, and they weren't at all sure that they wished to pollute their island with a munitions' factory.

'I can come back later if it's awkward just now, Father,' Roger said.

It was obvious that Sir Peter was in a bad mood, so the subject of Kate Christian's welfare was hardly likely to put him in a better one.

'No, you can stay,' he said, getting up and going over to the drinks' cabinet, poured himself a large brandy and soda. 'Care to join me?'

Roger didn't particularly want a drink before lunch, but he rightly guessed it politic to have one.

'That would be nice,' he said politely.

Sir Peter handed him a glass of the amber liquid.

'Cheers,' his father said, 'not that there's anything to be very cheerful about!' and he launched into a tirade against the Manx government.

'It's early days yet, Father,' Roger replied soothingly. 'Give them time. I'm sure they'll come around to your way of thinking, as it would help to deal with the unemployment problem.'

'I'm not bothered about that!' Sir Peter replied cynically. 'But it would make a lot of money when war breaks out, and that does interest me!'

'You're very sure that there's going to be a war.'

Sir Peter looked at his son impatiently.

'My dear fellow, it's more than obvious! I'm only glad that Damian and Winston are still at Eton, otherwise they might be dragged into the fray.'

Damian and Winston were Roger's two younger brothers, fourteen and eleven respectively. Roger noticed that his father hadn't bothered to mention the fact that he, Roger, would be called up. He smiled wryly. Well, no, he wouldn't. Damian was undoubtedly his father's favourite, so it would surely suit the old man if his eldest son could obligingly be knocked off in the war. But he mustn't speak such thoughts aloud, not when he was hoping to elicit some sympathy out of his father for

Kate Christian's predicament.

'I find it hard to believe that there'll be another world war,' Roger said. 'After all, wasn't the last one called the war to end all wars?'

Sir Peter snorted.

'You're so gullible, my lad! Sometimes I wonder whom you take after. One thing for sure, it certainly isn't me, or your lovely, but somewhat feather-brained mother, come to that!'

'I'm like my grandmother, your mother,' Roger said, and knew that it had been the right thing to say when his father's face softened.

'Yes, you are very like Mary was, Roger. She was so good, so gentle.'

Then his face hardened.

'And she was a woman! Such qualities are admirable in womankind, but you, you should be forgetting your art and trying to be a man!'

'She loved art, and I like to think that I've inherited her talent.'

'Oh, you've certainly done that. It's a pity that she had to die so young. She would have been very proud of your art exhibitions.'

'I wish she could have seen them.'

Sir Peter reached for the brandy decanter.

'Another?' he asked his son.

Roger, not wanting one at all, felt obliged to agree, but this would be the last. He would just have to plunge in about Kate quickly, because otherwise he knew that his hard-drinking father would have him intoxicated!

'Do you know, Father, that young woman, Katherine Christian, she reminded me a little of grandmother?'

Sir Peter frowned.

'Katherine Christian?'

Kate had already been totally obliterated from the older man's memory.

'The young woman who called just now. The one I saw and pretended to be you.'

Sir Peter threw back his head and laughed. He was subject to mercurial changes of mood, and the thought of his rather sobersides son impersonating him was very amusing.

'And how did you get on with her, son? Did she believe you were me?'

'Yes, I'm sure she did. I think she was a bit surprised that I . . . '

'Then she must be a gullible creature! But then, these locals often are.'

Roger was furious, and couldn't hide it.

'Kate seemed a very intelligent and spirited young lady!' he said hotly.

'My, my, lad, but she has made a big impression on you, hasn't she? She is the gardener chappie's daughter, I take it? Come to plead for Daddy's job to be reinstated, did she?'

'No, she did not! Although she made it clear that she considered your . . . or should I say my treatment of her father to be despicable, and I agree. You could at least have given the fellow more notice and let him stay in his cottage a while longer! After all, it's not as if there isn't plenty of room for your gardener and his wife

53

and children here, at least on a short-time basis. There's a lodge in the grounds he could use.'

'Oh, no, my lad, he's not having that!'

'May I ask why?'

His father cuffed him about the ears, but in a playful way. The brandy had mellowed Sir Peter's mood.

'You shouldn't ask, but you need to grow up, so I'll tell you why. The lodge is where I intend to entertain my . . . er . . . shall we say friends?'

Roger hadn't lived in a Paris garret flat and remained totally innocent.

'You mean your lady friends, of course. Aren't you keeping them a bit close to Mother?'

'Your mother doesn't care a jot as long as she gets her creature comforts! This, my lad, was a marriage of convenience, and it has worked out very well. Alicia and I jog along comfortably together. She understands me, and I her. But you do see why Roberts can't have the lodge?'

'Surely you haven't got women lined up already?'

Despite his good intentions, there was a sneer in Roger's voice.

'I've met several ladies on my various trips to the Isle of Man. When I'm ready for them to come, there'll be no shortage, of that I can assure you! In fact, I can probably fix you up, too, if you like!'

Sir Peter was being deliberately provocative, and Roger knew it. With difficulty, he held on to his temper.

'I don't think that there'll be any need for that, Father! As a matter of fact, I prefer to choose my own female companions! All right, keep the lodge for your women. You will anyway, but even so, Danny Roberts and his family are staying in the house now. Can't you give Kate's father an extension on his cottage? At least it would make things a little easier for the poor girl!'

'You do seem very concerned about Kate Christian. You're not imagining yourself falling in love with her or something crazy like that, are you?'

'Of course I'm not!' Roger retorted, rather too quickly. 'But I am sorry for her. I think that you've treated her father very shabbily, and it's caused misery for the whole family. She isn't a stupid girl. She was studying at the Clareville Secretarial School. She has ambitions. She wants to work as a stenographer for the government.'

'And how are her secretarial skills? Judging by the trouble I'm having so far with this poxy Manx government, I'll probably need to engage a secretary, at least part-time.'

This was promising, but Roger didn't want to appear too eager.

'I don't know, but she has been studying there and the place has a very good name, I believe. She also said that the principal was going to allow her to come in on a part-time basis, given the fact that she must now seek employment, since her father will have a cut in wages and . . . '

'Spare me all the gory details, do!' Sir

Peter implored. 'Can she type, do shorthand and put a letter together? That's what I want to know.'

'I'm sure she can. Anyway, I said that I'd think things over. Well, I had to do that, given the fact that she thought I was you. I asked her to come here tomorrow at around the same time as today, about ten, I think it was.'

'Ten o'clock on a Sunday morning? Still, never mind, you've intrigued me a little with your tales of Miss Katherine Christian. But this time, I'll see her, and ascertain the extent of her secretarial skills before I decide if I can offer her a position!'

Kate was nervous as she approached The Grange the following morning, at approximately quarter to ten. Would Sir Peter offer her a job? Certainly a live-in, part-time secretarial position would be wonderful, the answer to her prayers, yet she didn't want to get her hopes up. Hopes had a horrible way of dying, unfulfilled.

Sir Peter was a complete enigma — a

man she was sure she would hate, and yet whom she had liked, and, albeit reluctantly, if she was going to be truthful with herself, found attractive, too.

It would be nice to work in the same house as him, or would it? They were worlds apart. He was gentry, whereas she was poor, honest but poor. The rich were different and she, practical Kate Christian, would do very well to remember that.

Violet, the maid who had let Kate into The Grange the previous morning, greeted her once again.

'Good morning, miss.'

She was much more affable than the previous day, Kate noticed, and crossed her fingers momentarily. Surely that was a good sign. Servants usually knew which way the wind was blowing.

'Good morning.' Kate smiled apologetically. 'I'm sorry, I don't know your name, although now I come to think of it, your face does look familiar.'

'I'm Violet Costain, miss. My family

lives in King Street. You live in Parr Street, don't you? Wasn't your dad the head gardener here?'

'Yes, until Sir Peter dismissed him!'

'Don't fret, miss. The gentry are like that. Doesn't mean a thing to them, I'm afraid! It's nothing personal against your dad, well, it couldn't be, could it? Given the fact that he was such a good worker an' all. It's just Sir Peter has his own fellow, and, well, I think that they just imagine that their people are better because they bring them in from England.'

Kate smiled wanly.

'You're probably right, Violet. But please don't call me miss. If I get a job, I'll be a servant just as you are. Call me Kate, my friends do, and I'm hoping that you'll be one of them.'

'I will indeed, miss . . . er . . . I mean, Kate. I'd show you into the drawing-room, or one of those other fancy rooms so that you could wait in comfort for himself there, but I daren't. I wasn't given orders to do so, you see, and the way things are, I mean, not knowing whether you're going to have a job or whether her ladyship, when she comes, will insist on bringing her servants with her, well, I'll just have to leave you standing here lest I do the wrong thing. But once I tell him, he shouldn't be long, and I can ask him if he wants me to show you into his study or some such place.'

Violet came back a few minutes later.

'Good news or bad?' Kate asked.

'Good, I think.' Violet smiled at her. 'The master . . . he said that you're to wait for him in the drawing-room. I'm to take you there and you're to be served with morning coffee and cakes.'

Left alone, seated in the drawing-room, Kate flicked through copies of The Huntsman, while she waited for Sir Peter to come. It was boring, and, she thought, unpleasant reading, as she had always abhorred all forms of hunting. She threw the magazine away to the farthest corner of the settee. Well, although he had seemed kind and gentle, obviously, Sir Peter Grenville was a self-centred, cruel person who had tricked her into believing that he was a thoughtful and civilised human being.

Sir Peter entered the room some half an hour later. Kate, who had been looking out of the window, turned around, and then, seeing him, seeing that he was a man in his late forties or maybe early fifties, it was impossible to tell, was bewildered.

'Who are you?' she asked. 'I'm waiting to see Sir Peter Grenville.'

He stood there, handsome in his way, if one disregarded the bags under his eyes, the thinning dark hair, the stomach which was beginning to be corpulent.

'I'm Sir Peter Grenville,' he said, his voice laced with amusement. 'You spoke to my son yesterday. He's a nice enough chap, but totally unworldly I'm afraid!'

His cat-like eyes bored into hers.

'But I'm quite sure that we're soon

going to understand one another, aren't we, Miss Christian, daughter of the gardener?'

Kate shook her head, her eyes dilated. Surely she was in a nightmare. But, no, this was for real. Yesterday had been the fairy tale!

4

'You look as if something singularly unpleasant has occurred,' Sir Peter commented, a mocking note in his voice. 'Am I to take it that you prefer my rather wimpish son to myself?'

Kate was sure that she did, but she could scarcely say that to the owner of The Grange. Anyway, what had Sir Peter's son been up to, playing a trick like that on her? It was hardly the kindest thing to do. Sir Peter was watching her like a cat eyeing up a mouse.

'I see you've had coffee. Were the cakes not to your liking?'

'They looked lovely, but I wasn't hungry. Anyway, I understand that I was to come here to see if you have any employment for me, not a social call!'

She looked at him directly then, and Sir Peter chuckled. This was a fiery piece, and very attractive, too. She would make a worthy addition to the ladies he planned to have visit him at the lodge. But she looked as if she would play hard to get. Still, a challenge was always interesting.

'I may well be able to offer you employment, Katherine Christian. My son tells me that you have been attending secretarial college. How advanced are you with your studies?'

'I can type quite quickly, and I have a speed of eighty words per minute for shorthand at the present time. The principal, Mrs Rogers, has told me that I am one of the most promising pupils whom she has taught.'

'Indeed? Well, if you're telling the truth, that is most encouraging.'

Kate's eyes blazed at him, as she said, 'I always tell the truth, Sir Peter!'

'I'm very pleased to hear it, for it's a rare commodity nowadays! But I can easily ring your principal and find out. Mrs Rogers, you say?'

Kate nodded mutely.

'And the school is called?'

He was making notes as he spoke.

'It's the Clareville Secretarial College, the only one in Douglas.'

'Then if you will excuse me for a few moments, I will ring her right away.'

He inclined his head, and then left the room, leaving Kate as if turned to stone. She didn't know what to make of Sir Peter, but she didn't like him. Still, if he was prepared to employ her, well, she would be foolish not to give it a try. After all, she would be getting further practice in her secretarial work, something which she wanted to do far more than domestic or factory work.

Sir Peter was back within five minutes.

'She spoke of you in glowing terms,' he informed Kate, smiling at her, although the smile didn't reach his eyes, which remained wary and cat-like. 'In fact, my dear, you've been too modest. She told me that you are the most promising student she has ever taught, and that you also have knowledge of book-keeping, something else which will be useful to me. Therefore, I am quite prepared to take you on. You can have a room here, all found, and I will initially require your services three days a week. These may not be the same days each week. It will depend whether I am on or off the island, and on the work load. She is happy for you to attend your college on the other two days. She also said that you needn't worry about payment, but I think that as long as you prove satisfactory, her fees for the two days could be met as part of your salary. I'll pay you fifteen shillings a week.'

Fifteen shillings a week! It was more than fair, particularly given the fact that he had also said that he would pay her fees to Mrs Rogers, if she was satisfactory, and she would have free accommodation and food. Certainly, she seemed to have fallen on her feet.

'That's very kind of you, sir, thank you,' she said.

66

He smiled.

'Right then, Miss Christian, I'll have one of my men help you bring your things over here this afternoon, if that is satisfactory to you. That will give you the rest of the day to settle in here, and then you will be ready to start work tomorrow.'

He stood up. Clearly the interview was at an end. Kate did likewise. He held out his hand, and Kate took it. His hand was icy cold, despite the fact that the room was warm.

'You can find your own way out, I trust?'

So, he wasn't going to escort her off the premises, as his son had done. Well, she hadn't expected him to. Sir Peter definitely had the air of a man who was lord of the manor. Still, he had made her a more than fair offer, so despite an instinctive dislike of the man, Kate knew that she should be feeling kindly disposed towards him.

'Certainly, sir. What time is your man likely to call to collect my belongings?'

'Two o'clock. That should give you adequate time to make your preparations.'

It was only after Kate had left The Grange and was walking back home to the little terraced house in Parr Street that a sudden thought struck her. What on earth was she going to tell her parents about her new plans? She knew that both of them would be up in arms at her intention of working part-time for Sir Peter, and going to live in his house.

She sighed. Oh, well, much as she didn't like it, she supposed that for now she would have to tell a white lie, and pretend that the manservant from The Grange had come from the fictitious Cathy's house. But wouldn't her father recognise the man? After all, he had likely been in the employ of Mr Quilliam, would be a local man and certainly known to her father.

Kate bit her bottom lip, as she wondered what to do. Could she meet him outside, perhaps a little way along the street? If she watched out for him coming, that shouldn't be too much of a problem, and it was quite feasible that the imaginary Cathy and her family would wish Kate to move in today, given the fact that the Christians were due to leave their home the following day. And her parents would be busy. More than likely, they would be engaged in moving their own belongings to their respective destinations.

Comforted, she went home with a lighter heart.

Kate was right. Number Two Parr Street was in chaos. Margaret was clearly upset as she packed her belongings, the girls struggling to help her, whilst Kate's father, his face grim, was struggling to get his own belongings together.

'I'll help you in a moment, Mum,' Kate said, giving her mother a quick hug. 'But I need to get my things packed first. Cathy Cregeen's family is sending someone over to collect my things and take them to their house.

They think it will be better if I move in today.'

'Aye, love, you're right.'

It was her father, Walter, who answered. Then he scratched his head.

'Mind, they must have some money, these Cregeens, to be able to send someone over for your stuff. I was expecting to bring it over myself. Where did you say they live?'

Kate hadn't, actually, and she paused momentarily, before coming up with, 'They live in Devonshire Road. As you know, it's not too far from here.'

Her father smiled, a smile laced with bitterness.

'Oh, aye, well, I suppose they would live in the better part of town! Banker you said her father was, didn't you?'

'Yes.'

Kate turned away then. Having to lie to her parents, her good, honest parents, was taking its toll of her. Yet what else could she do? She would tell them the truth just as soon as she could, but she knew that right now just wasn't that time.

'I'll go upstairs and get my things together, then I'll give you a hand,' she said, in a voice which, even to her own ears, sounded slightly guttural.

She hurried out of the room and upstairs to the tiny room which had at least been her own for a number of years now, and rummaged through the chipped and stained, old wardrobe.

It was just gone twenty to two when Kate decided she had better make her way to the top of Parr Street in case the man Sir Peter sent was early. Anyway, Parr Street was so narrow that it was impossible to get any sort of a vehicle down it, and she imagined that the man would have some sort of transport. This proved to be a good reason to give to Kate's parents, too.

'Well, of course, you must wait at the top of the street, love,' her mother said. 'You don't want to put these good people to any more trouble.'

Then it was hugs and kisses, and

promises to visit Auntie Elsie's and Uncle Fred's.

'And I'll call over at Farmer Kelly's, Pa,' Kate said.

'Leave it a few days first, love. It's not that I don't want to see you,' he added hastily, as he saw her crestfallen face, 'but I'll need a few days to settle in, find my feet, so to speak.'

What he really meant was that he wanted to sound out the lie of the land before he started inviting visitors, even his favourite daughter. Kate guessed this was the reason, but wisely refrained from making any comment.

'I'll come and see you and the girls first, Mum,' she told her mother, 'and you can tell me when it's OK to visit Dad.'

She smiled, although she suddenly felt close to tears. It was the first time that her family would be separated, and it was hard.

'Well, I'd best be off. I don't want to keep Sir . . . I mean Cathy's parents' man waiting. Goodbye, Dad, Mum. I'm sure everything will be just fine.'

Then she kissed her two sisters.

' 'Bye, kids, and take care of Mum.'

'I will,' little Meg said solemnly.

Jessie just clung to her big sister, which made things all the harder.

'What did you mean when you said sir just then?'

Her father was frowning. Kate put Jessie from her gently.

'I really didn't mean anything. I suppose that I was thinking about Sir Peter, blaming him for this, and it came out kind of muddled.'

Her father nodded.

'Aye, well, the blackguard has a lot to answer for, that's true enough! But don't go worrying your pretty little head about him. The chances are that you'll never lay eyes on him, and thankful I am that you won't, either, because I wouldn't trust the fellow as far as I could throw him! Now, be off with you lass, and take care.'

Kate turned away. She didn't trust herself to speak.

Sir Peter's man, Robbie Karran, whom Kate knew by sight, but not to speak to, turned up in a very posh Bentley about five minutes after she arrived at the top of the street. He jumped out of the car, a handsome young man with blond, curly hair and laughing blue eyes.

'I thought you'd probably be waiting here, Miss Christian, so I decided to come along a bit on the early side.'

As he spoke, he lifted her battered suitcase and put it in the boot.

'Right then, in you get,' he said, smiling down at her from his six-feet height, which was some six inches taller than Kate.

'Although it's summer, it's cold.'

'It's certainly got a nip in the air,' she agreed, as she climbed into the car, the first time that she'd ever been in one, and Robbie closed the door behind her, before going over to the other side and climbing in beside her.

'Where did you learn to drive?' she asked, as he put the car into gear and reversed into Clarke Street, the adjoining street to Parr Street.

'On my dad's farm,' he replied. 'The old man has a couple of vans. He uses one for his milk round. I think he hoped I'd go into the family business, which means either farming or doing a milk round, but I'm sorry to say that neither appealed much to me. I've always been far more interested in cars.'

'You were working for Mr Quilliam, weren't you?'

'Yes, for the past three years now I've been his chauffeur-cum-mechanic. I'm just thankful that Sir Peter kept me on. I thought he might have brought some fellow from England in like he did with the gardener and the butler.'

He put a hand to his forehead.

'Trust me to put my big foot in it! I'm sorry, Kate . . . er . . . I mean, Miss Christian. I do know about your dad, and I'm truly sorry. It was a lousy thing to do, but then, although I don't know him that well, I would guess Sir Peter is as hard as nails!'

'There's no need for you to call me Miss Christian. Kate will do very well,' Kate said with a smile, for Robbie Karran seemed a very pleasant young man. 'Yes, Sir Peter did treat my father shabbily, and although I know I should be grateful to him for giving me a job, I can't really say that I took to him. Why do you say he's as hard as nails?'

'Well, it wasn't just your dad he got rid of you know. He sacked poor old Nellie Faragher, the cook, and brought some French chef in to take her place. She was really upset, seeing as how she'd worked at The Grange since she was a lass of thirteen. Then there was old Bill Crebbin, who acted as Mr Quilliam's butler-cum-handyman. Mr Quilliam didn't really stand on ceremony enough to actually have a butler as such. Well, Bill was told he could stay on as an odd-job man, but that he wouldn't be needed for anything else, for His Lordship brought his own fellow with him, and a right snob Worthington is, too! I wonder that he and Sir Peter aren't fighting like cat and dog, because honestly, Worthington is as snotty-nosed as they come. Speaks as if he's got a handful of plums in his mouth.'

'What did Bill Crebbin do?' Kate asked.

She knew the old man, and had always found him very kind. When she'd been a little lass, and gone to visit her father at The Grange, Bill had always had sweets or chocolates for her.

'He left,' Robbie said, his mouth tight. 'Well, what else could he do? If he'd have stayed on, he'd have been treated like dirt, and the old fellow knew it! No, he was in his late sixties, so at least he'll get some money out of this miserly government, but still, he was sad to go. Like Nellie, he'd been at The Grange since he was a lad.'

Kate sighed.

'It does seem very hard.'

Then she gave a mirthless laugh.

'But I suppose Sir Peter doesn't see any harm in it. I imagine that the likes of him would tend to think of us locals as little better than savages!'

Robbie threw her a quick look, and then concentrated on his driving. So she was bitter about the situation. Well, small wonder, but why had Sir Peter employed her? Oh, he knew that she was studying at that secretarial place, but then, there were loads of people out of work. If His Lordship, as Robbie disparagingly called his boss, wanted a secretary, then he need only telephone the local labour exchange, and no doubt there'd be tons of them clamouring after the work. So why take on Walter Christian's daughter when he'd had trouble with the father, and the lass was only half-trained?

Robbie smiled grimly. He had a notion he could guess why. Sir Peter was a womaniser, of that he was sure, and Kate Christian was a very attractive young woman. Robbie had gone quiet, and after his initial friendliness, Kate wondered why. Had she somehow said something to upset him?

'There's nothing wrong, is there?' she asked tentatively.

'No, sorry, Kate, I was wool-gathering, miles away, I was!'

But he wasn't about to tell her what he'd been thinking.

Instead, he said, 'Sir Peter is going to take time to get used to our ways, I'm afraid. That is, if he ever does! He's the spit of a caricature of an English gentleman, you know the sort, hunting shooting, fishing.'

And chasing the women, he thought, but didn't say.

'He's certainly not a very appealing character,' Kate said, disapproval evident in her tone. 'I met his son, too, you know.'

She turned and looked out of the window, hesitated. What would she say about Sir Peter's son? He had tricked her, yes, and yet . . . and yet . . .

Robbie was interested.

'Oh, you have, have you? And how did that come about? He's a poet, is young Mr Roger, and tends to keep himself pretty much to himself. Not his father's type. The two of them often row.'

'He pretended to be his father,' Kate said briefly, and saw that Robbie was curious.

By this time, however, they were in the long drive which led to The Grange. There wasn't time to go into details, and Robbie knew it.

'You must tell me later,' he said. 'It sounds interesting.'

'I probably will,' Kate said, as Robbie stopped the car outside the house and, going over to her side of the car, helped her out.

'You'd better!' he said, opening the boot and taking out her case.

Kate stiffened, and he cursed himself once again for putting his foot in it. That was the wrong way to approach Kate Christian, and he wanted to approach her. He'd been watching her for some time now, and wondering if he'd ever get the opportunity, and the nerve, to ask her for a date.

5

Violet, the maidservant who had first greeted Kate at The Grange, showed her up to her bedroom, a surprisingly large and airy room on the second floor, and then helped Kate to unpack her few belongings. There was not much in the way of clothes, but a fair amount of books. Kate was clearly very clever, and Violet was impressed.

'I hope that you're going to be happy here, miss,' she said. 'I'm right glad that you're here, you know, because I reckon, well, that us islanders should be sticking together like and . . . '

Kate smiled. Now that she was being herself, Violet was quite amusing, but she mustn't stand on ceremony, not with her.

'Violet, I thought I told you before that you mustn't call me Miss Christian. It's much too formal, and it makes me feel like an old woman, and I'm probably only about the same age as you.'

'I'm sorry, Miss . . . er . . . I mean, Kate! It's just that I'm the maid of all work, like, whereas you're the master's secretary and so . . .'

Kate interrupted her again.

'He isn't the master! He's a human being, just as we are! He may have a title, but that doesn't mean to say he's a god to be bowed and scraped to!'

Kate was irritated by Violet's obvious awe of her employer, and didn't hear the knock at the door, or it opening, and Roger Grenville standing just inside the room. He looked amused, and she felt decidedly silly. Just how much had the master's son heard?

'I'm sorry, I didn't mean to intrude,' he was saying now, spreading his hands in an apologetic way. 'I did knock, you know!'

Violet was decidedly ill at ease.

'If you'll excuse me, sir, I've work I should be attending to,' she said, and hurried past him, not waiting to see whether he objected or not.

'Oh, dear,' he said. 'I'm afraid I seem to have frightened her, although why that should be I don't know. I've always spoken kindly to her and . . . '

'Perhaps it's because you remind her of your father!' Kate said tersely.

Roger wasn't much like his father in looks or nature, as far as she could tell, but he had annoyed her. He looked horrified at what she'd said.

'I can't think why,' he said, shaking his head. 'I know that I favour my mother in looks, and I'm like his mother in ways so . . . '

Kate gave an exasperated smile.

'It's all right, I didn't mean it! I was just annoyed that I didn't hear you come in, and I'm also cross about that little charade you played on me, pretending to be your father! Why did you do it?'

Roger looked distinctly abashed.

'I honestly don't know,' he admitted. 'I suppose I felt guilty about your father, although I couldn't have done anything about it. The old man never listens to me, thinks I'm a dreamer, and he prefers men of action. But I wanted to see you anyway. I suppose I was curious, and I admired you for having the guts to come to The Grange and face up to my father.'

Kate smiled.

'Well, at least you're truthful, something which I think your father might not be and . . . '

She broke off. Oh, no! What was she saying to her employer's son? She hadn't even started work here yet, and even if Roger Grenville didn't get on well with his father, she didn't know him well enough to be talking to him like this.

'I'm sorry,' she said. 'I shouldn't have said that.'

'Don't worry, I'm not about to run off and tell him! Anyway, you've probably got a point. My father does tend to twist things a bit if it suits his purpose. But I didn't come here to talk about him. I thought you might like to take a tour of the house, and as it's not raining, we can have a look at the gardens, too, if you like. We don't eat until half past seven, so you've plenty of time, and Father won't need you today.'

He was trying to be friendly, and Kate felt in need of a friend.

'That would be nice, I'd like that.' She smiled. 'It's probably going to help me a lot, too, because although I've been here in the past, I never got beyond the kitchen and it looks as if it's quite a big place.'

'Oh, it is. It's one of the largest houses on the Isle of Man, actually. It was built at the time of the Duke of Atholl, the Governor of the island in the eighteenth century. He lived in the Castle Mona, that big hotel on the promenade.'

'Yes, I know,' Kate said rather dryly.

Roger shook his head.

'Sorry! Here I am trying to give you a history lesson, and you're the Manx lady and I'm the incomer!'

'It's nice that you've taken the time to find out things about the island,' she replied. 'At least it shows that you're interested in it.'

'I am interested,' he said sincerely. 'I think it's a beautiful place, so peaceful after London, but I've never been a city person. I spent time in Paris, and I enjoyed that, mainly because it helped my art so much and . . . '

He broke off, looking acutely embarrassed.

'Sorry, I don't want to bore you.'

Kate smiled.

'But you're not boring me. I'm interested. It must be wonderful to travel.'

It was her turn to look embarrassed as she added, 'I'm afraid I've only ever been on a day-trip to Liverpool, and even that was two years ago now. And you said about art. Are you an artist?'

'I have had a couple of exhibitions, and was lucky enough to sell some paintings, but I'm no Monet!'

'You must be very good to have had

exhibitions of your work and sold some of it,' Kate replied.

Certainly, Roger Grenville seemed nothing like his father. She couldn't imagine the worldly Sir Peter painting. He would surely consider it a complete and utter waste of time.

'My grandmother was an artist, my father's mother, surprisingly. My father doesn't take after her, though. He favours his father. My grandfather was a bluff, heavy-set man with a florid complexion. I think I was a bit afraid of him. He seemed so big, so boisterous! But my grandmother, well, to be honest, I could never understand what she saw in him, but then, I suppose that hers was an arranged marriage. I don't think they were very happy.'

Kate laid a comforting hand on Roger's arm.

'Don't worry about it,' she said soothingly. 'The past is over. I never think it helps too much to dwell upon it.'

'No, you're right,' he agreed, thinking

how sensitive and understanding she was. 'But I should be showing you around the house like I said, and not standing here boring you to death with talk of my forebears.'

'It would be interesting to have a look around the house.'

She had been a bit concerned about them being alone together in the bedroom. Oh, there was nothing whatsoever in it, but would other people see it like that? Even Violet, who had fled from the room so quickly, would think it strange that Kate was alone with her employer's son in her bedroom.

'But I think it might be an idea if you took me on the grand tour, so to speak. As I said before, I've a hopeless sense of direction. At least it will stop me from getting lost!'

'Then shall we go, mademoiselle?' he said, giving her a mock, courtly bow. 'Would mam'selle care to take my arm?'

'No, mam'selle wouldn't!' she retorted,

not so much that she was averse to the suggestion, but she was horrified at the thought that Sir Peter might see them, and goodness knows what conclusions he would jump to then.

The Grange was a fascinating old house with a fascinating history. Roger had obviously studied the facts, because he certainly knew more about its history than she did. He was also a good, interesting teacher, as he explained the various family photographs which adorned the wall leading down the staircase, and told her musing anecdotes of the house's past. Apparently, it had been owned by a Manxman who had made a fortune as a privateer in the Caribbean. The house had been a smuggler's den, a safe refuge for numerous crates of illicit brandy brought in from France.

'So you see,' Roger said, with a faintly cynical smile, 'there were plenty of rogues about even in those days.'

'I'm not surprised!' Kate returned. 'After all, we are supposed to be civilised now. These poor souls were around in the eighteenth century. We shouldn't expect too much of them!'

'Nothing has really changed though, has it?' he said. 'Human nature being what it is, we will always have unscrupulous people to contend with!'

They were looking at a portrait of the privateer's third wife, a fiery Spanish piece with jet black hair and dangling earrings.

'Ah, so you're admiring Lola.'

The voice behind them made both Kate and Roger start visibly. It was Sir Peter, and, moving stealthily, they hadn't heard him approach.

'A fine-looking woman, I'm sure you'll agree. Apparently, she was the mistress of one of the Spanish kings before she married old Sir Ranulf Corrin. And a merry dance she led him, if the history books are to be believed!'

'Father, I didn't hear you.'

Roger immediately looked ill at ease, and Kate found her heart going out to him. He obviously wasn't at all at home with his father.

'No, well, you wouldn't, would you?' Sir Peter said, with an enigmatic smile. 'Weren't you surprised by my knowledge of history, Sonny Jim? It isn't just you who can study facts about this house, you know!'

'It's a beautiful place, you must be very proud of it,' Kate said quickly.

There was definite friction in the air, and she didn't like it. It made her feel decidedly uncomfortable.

'The house is all right,' Sir Peter said, without much interest, 'but the social life on the island leaves a lot to be desired! Still, no doubt it will improve once your mother deigns to come, Roger.'

He smiled at Kate, but there was no warmth in the smile.

'Well, I'll leave you once again in my son's most capable hands, my dear, and look forward to seeing you at dinner. You will be dining with us en famille unless we're entertaining.'

He nodded at his son and walked off. Roger looked angry.

'Why does he always have to sound so patronising!'

'Well, I am just a servant, after all, Mr Grenville.'

'What dated nonsense! This is 1939, not 1539! You're an employee.'

She inclined her head.

'Maybe so, but I'm still paid to do a job, and I'm living in. I would imagine that to your father's mind that would put me in the servant category!'

'My father just likes being irritating. Try to ignore him,' Roger replied. 'And there's no need for you to call me Mr Grenville, either. I'd be much happier if you'd call me Roger.'

'And will your father approve of that?'

'I've no idea, and I certainly couldn't care less! I'm over twenty-one, a man. It isn't up to him.'

'I'll call you Roger in private,' Kate said, relenting a bit. 'But I think it's probably better for me to say Mr

Grenville in company.'

She smiled to soften her words.

'After all, I do need this job you know!'

'As you wish,' he replied, but he was tight-lipped, and obviously the arrangement didn't really satisfy him. 'Well, if you've seen enough of the house to be going on with, we may as well take a look outside while it's still fine. It's forecast rain for tonight.'

Kate inclined her head, but, somehow, her tour of the house and garden had been spoiled. It was hard to say exactly why. Sir Peter hadn't really done anything, yet there was something about the man. Oh, well, perhaps he was just missing his wife and he would be better when Lady Grenville came to live on the island.

In fact, Lady Alicia came to Douglas three days later.

Kate had settled into life at The Grange reasonably well. Sir Peter wasn't the easiest of employers, but then, she hadn't expected him to be. He was angry with the Manx government for refusing him permission to start up a munitions' factory, and most of Kate's work was bombarding them with letters which stated Sir Peter's case eloquently, although Kate doubted that his intentions were as honourable as he made them out to be.

'My wife is sailing on The Snaefell today,' Sir Peter announced abruptly, tossing a piece of paper to one side and looking at Kate.

'Will you be going to meet her?'

Sir Peter looked at Kate as if she was quite mad.

'No, of course not! I'll leave that to young Karran. That's what he's paid for when all's said and done!'

Kate lowered her eyes so that Sir Peter wouldn't be able to read the expression in them.

'Of course, sir,' she murmured demurely.

'Look at me when I'm talking to you!'

Kate did so, she was so startled by his

sudden command. Sir Peter laughed harshly.

'That's better! I hate milksops!'

'Sir, I really don't think that this conversation is furthering our work.'

'No, by jove, it isn't!' he agreed. 'But it's a damn sight more interesting, nonetheless!'

Kate was saved by a knock at the door, which opened before Sir Peter had a chance to say anything.

'What do you want?' he said and scowled at his son, his voice decidedly irritable. 'Can't you see that I'm busy?'

Roger gave his father a withering look.

'Have you forgotten that Mother will be arriving in half an hour? Shouldn't you be going to meet her?'

'Cheeky young whippersnapper! Since when did I have to go running after your mother? Karran can fetch her!'

Roger turned to Kate.

'Come, Kate, we'll go with Robbie to meet my mother.'

Kate hesitated. This was a difficult situation. She would rather go with Roger, not because she was particularly bothered about seeing Lady Grenville, but she did feel that she would like to get away from the lady's husband, whose present mood was beginning to unnerve her.

'Are you telling my secretary what to do?'

Sir Peter stood up, his stance belligerent.

'Yes.'

Sir Peter inclined his head, his face enigmatic.

'Very well, if that is what you wish, who am I to stand in your way?'

Kate stood up and moved towards the door.

'Thank you, Sir Peter,' she said, by way of an afterthought.

'No need, my dear,' he replied cynically. 'It's rather interesting to see my son endeavouring to be a man for once!'

'He's intolerable!' Roger stormed, as

they made their way from The Grange down to the quayside where The Snaefell would dock.

Kate shook her head. She could tell from his attitude that Robbie Karran was listening. Now wasn't the time to discuss Sir Peter's foibles.

'What's your mother like?' Kate asked instead.

'My mother, like my father, is difficult,' he admitted frankly. 'But she's harmless. Unless her make-up doesn't go on properly, she's very pleasant to everyone.'

Kate laughed.

'That sounds very cynical!'

He shrugged.

'It isn't meant to be, honestly. No, really it's just a statement of fact.'

He tapped Robbie on the shoulder.

'OK, Rob, I know you're listening. You've met my mother. What's your opinion of her?'

Poor Robbie was horribly ill at ease as he said, 'Sir, Lady Alicia is a most charming lady. I couldn't possibly say anything else!'

'Come on, Robbie, there's no need for you to be diffident. You know my father isn't here!'

But Robbie refused to be drawn. Kate agreed with him. After all, if not a servant, as Roger kept insisting, they were paid employees of Sir Peter Grenville, and, therefore, had to watch their etiquette. They weren't going to be mere sport for the gentry.

6

'OK, Robbie, I'm sorry,' Roger said, as the latter parked Sir Peter's car as near to the landing stage as possible. 'I shouldn't have asked you to comment on my mother, it wasn't fair. It's my fault for having difficult parents, but that's no excuse for involving other people.'

Robbie's voice was stiff as he said, 'That's your prerogative, sir.'

Roger smiled. So Robbie had his pride. Well, he wasn't too surprised, and there was their obvious mutual interest in Kate Christian, which made them adversaries although he had nothing at all against his father's chauffeur, in fact, he really quite liked the man.

The Snaefell was wending her way into Douglas harbour, and would soon be docking, and the lovely, if slightly addle-brained Lady Grenville would soon be arriving.

'Come on, Kate, she'll be in in a minute. We'd better wait by the ship so that mother will see us.'

Kate looked a little nervous.

'Wouldn't it be better if you went on your own? She won't be expecting to see me with you and . . . '

'Rubbish!' he interrupted, rather rudely, but it did have the effect of keeping her quiet.

'All right then,' Kate said, weakly, feeling that her life was suddenly out of control.

What was this Society lady going to think of her son meeting her with a servant . . . no, she quickly corrected herself, an employee?

Kate, you're too downtrodden, she said to herself! You tell other people that it's the twentieth century, so act as if you think it is so yourself! You're as good as anyone else. Just because they've got more money it doesn't make them better people, so just go out there and face her!

Roger was looking amused.

'Kate, are you suffering some inner turmoil? You certainly look as if you are! Don't worry, Mother won't mind you being here, in fact, she'll be pleased that I've got a young lady in tow. So, come on! What she won't appreciate is being kept waiting!'

So that's what she was, a young lady in tow, whatever that meant. Kate didn't think it sounded very flattering, but she had no time to dwell on it, as Roger grabbed hold of her hand and literally pulled her out of the car, Robbie looking very disapproving.

Lady Grenville disembarked from the ferry a few minutes later. As she came down the gangway, Kate gasped, for she was an exceptionally beautiful woman with dark auburn hair cut in the latest style and the most fashionable clothes Kate had ever seen.

'Rog, darling!'

Lady Grenville threw her arms around her son's neck, and he hugged her, almost lifting her off the ground.

'It's marvellous to see you, precious!' she exclaimed, but, at the same time, she was disentangling herself from Roger's arms, clearly worried that her hair would be disturbed, or her lovely clothes ruffled. Then she noticed Kate, who had been cringing into herself, almost as if she was trying to make herself invisible.

'And who is this? Who is your little friend?'

At five foot six, Kate was fairly tall, but Lady Grenville wasn't speaking literally, being given to exaggeration and affections. Roger smiled.

'Miss Katherine Christian, a local young lady who has kindly agreed to help Father out with secretarial work.'

That was a nice, if not entirely truthful way of summing up the situation, Kate thought.

'My dear, it's lovely to see you,' Lady Grenville said, extending her hand.

Kate took it, and murmured, 'As I am to see you, Your Ladyship. I trust you had a pleasant crossing?'

Lady Grenville shrugged.

'As pleasant as these things can be. My cabin was tolerable, and the waiter efficient, but please, don't call me Your Ladyship. It's far too formal altogether and makes me sound positively old! Call me Lady Alicia. At least that sounds more human. Gracious, but it's cold standing around here!'

She looked about her with an air of distaste.

'Screeching seagulls and old Victorian guest houses! Good grief! What was your father thinking of when he decided to buy a house in this backwoods? I just know that I'm going to miss London terribly!'

'You don't know anything of the sort yet, Mother. You've only ever been here once before, and that was only for a few days. Give the place a chance. It can take a bit of time to settle into island life, but it is a very beautiful island. I'm sure you'll find it so when you've been here for a while.'

Lady Grenville looked far from

convinced, but she smiled as she linked her arm through her son's.

'Oh, well, I suppose you find the countryside appealing for your art work, although there'll be nowhere for you to exhibit it here.'

'There is an art society, and some of the members are very talented.'

Lady Grenville lifted a delicately-arched eyebrow.

'Really? You do surprise me!' Then her voice became petulant, as she added, 'Where's the chauffeur chappie? I'm freezing to death out here, despite having worn an outfit which I would never have dreamed of wearing until late autumn in London!'

'Robbie parked as near to the jetty as he could,' Roger assured her. 'The Bentley is just over here.'

And they moved towards the car, Kate trailing in their wake, feeling singularly out of place. Roger's mother had been pleasant enough to her, she supposed, but then, Roger had made it sound as if she, Kate, was doing Sir

Peter a favour by helping out with his secretarial work, rather than the truth, that she was a paid employee whose need of the money was great.

Kate sighed. She and Roger Grenville were worlds apart. Perhaps she shouldn't have accepted Sir Peter's offer, tempting as it had been, for surely it was foolish for her to be seeing Roger every day. She knew that she was most definitely attracted to him.

Kate was coming back from secretarial college the following day, her head bent against the persistent drizzle, when a car pulled up beside her, the door was flung open and Robbie's cheerful voice called.

'Come on, Kate, get in.'

Kate was glad to do so. It hadn't been raining when she had set out that morning, in fact, it had been quite sunny, but she should have had the sense to have brought a coat with her. Island weather was notoriously fickle, and as an islander, she knew that, but she'd been in a hurry after a disturbed night's sleep. She flushed, as she remembered that it was thoughts of Roger Grenville which had caused her insomnia.

Robbie looked at Kate and laughed.

'You look like a half-drowned rat!' he exclaimed cheerfully.

'Well, thank you very much!' she replied, pretending to be huffy.

'I like half-drowned rats,' he said, smiling at her as he started up the car.

'Strange taste you've got!' Kate said, laughing.

'Well, it does depend on the particular half-drowned rat, of course!' he teased, then, his tone more serious, he said, 'I've another three quarters of an hour to kill before I collect Lady Grenville from the hairdresser's, so what do you say that we have a hot drink?'

Kate, being so wet, did feel chilled.

'OK, then,' she agreed, 'but fancy Lady Alicia going to a local hairdresser's salon. I would have thought she'd have wanted someone to come to the house.'

'I think she thought it would be novel, well, that was her word, not mine, to try out one of the local places.'

'Sizing up the natives, eh?'

'Yes, I suppose you could call it that, and although she's a damned good-looking lady, she's a spoiled one, is the mistress. Still, she's a lot more pleasant than himself.'

'I take it you mean Sir Peter.'

Robbie nodded.

'Cussed blighter! And no better than he should be, neither! Not in any way, that is! At least Her Ladyship means no real harm.'

'I take it you don't like him.'

'I don't and that's a fact but, he pays the wages, so, being a working man, and liking cars, well, I just put up with him.'

By this time, Robbie had parked the car and got out and went round to Kate's side of the car, and opened the door for her. She got out, and smiled at him teasingly.

'Thank you, kind sir. You're the perfect gentleman!'

'It's comes naturally,' Robbie agreed with a teasing smile.

Inside the tearoom, Robbie ordered a cream tea.

'Are you sure we've got time for all this?' Kate asked, slightly worried. 'Lady Alicia will hardly expect me to be there when you go to meet her.'

'I don't know that she'd bother.'

'Oh, no, I'd be embarrassed!'

Robbie looked at Kate for a moment or two, and then nodded.

'Aye, you're probably right,' he agreed, but he couldn't help but feel a bit disappointed, nonetheless.

He'd been hoping that Kate would have come with him when he met the mistress from the hairdresser's. That way, Her Ladyship might have thought that he and Kate, her husband's secretary, were an item, and that's what he wanted them to be. But he wasn't going to show that he was disappointed. He guessed rightly that that wouldn't be the way to handle Kate.

'I'll drop you back there first! It's only five or ten minutes away, and then go for Her Ladyship.'

Then he hesitated. He wanted to ask Kate out, but he didn't want to scare her off. Oh, well, there was nowt for it but to plunge in and ask her.

'Kate, there's a film that's supposed to be really good on at the Odeon. Would you come and see it with me? T'ain't much fun going to the pictures on your own. Nobody to discuss the film with, like.'

Kate smiled to herself. She had been wondering if Robbie was interested in her, now this seemed to confirm that he was. Well, she shouldn't really lead him on if she couldn't return his feelings, not that she didn't like him. She did, he was a likeable fellow, but Roger . . . no! She was being a fool. Roger Grenville was gentry and she and Robbie were working-class.

'What's the film?' she asked Robbie, smiling at him.

'It's a love story, Interlude in Paris. Jean Harlow and Clark Gable are in it, so I think it should be pretty good.'

'All right then. When do you want to go?'

She had agreed! Robbie couldn't keep the grin off his face.

'Well, now, work permitting, that would be up to you.'

'I can probably go any evening. It's rare for Sir Peter to want any secretarial work done in the evenings. Some nights I have to study with exams coming up in July.'

'I wouldn't want to get in the way of your studies,' he assured her. 'I admire you a lot for the way in which you're trying to better yourself.'

Then he looked embarrassed. Would she be offended at a remark like that? But no, Kate was smiling at him, and it was like a sudden burst of sunshine on a cloudy day.

'I can go tomorrow night, if that suits

you,' Kate said, taking pity on him.

'Yes, just great! Sir Peter will probably let me take the car. He's not too bad in that way. Well, he will if he doesn't want to use it himself, and if he does, well, the likelihood is that he'll want my services, too. He can drive, but he rarely chooses to do so.'

'Well, he won't, will he, when he's paying you to drive him places?' Kate replied, with a touch of cynicism. 'But don't worry, Robbie, if you can't make it for tomorrow, then I'll come with you another night.'

Then she looked at her watch.

'But we'd best be going soon, if you're not to keep Lady Alicia waiting.'

'Yes, you're right.'

Robbie finished his tea, and went over to the pay desk to settle up.

'We'll say tomorrow then,' Robbie said, as he dropped Kate off outside The Grange. 'Any change, and I'll let you know.'

'That's fine, Robbie.'

Kate's hand was on the door handle,

but taking her totally by surprise, Robbie suddenly leaned over and kissed her cheek.

'Sorry,' he said, looking bashful. 'It was just instinctive like!'

Kate couldn't really be angry, for it had been a harmless enough gesture.

'That's all right,' she said, this time letting herself out of the car, although she could see that he was starting to get out to come round and open the door for her. 'But don't push your luck too far!'

Then, laughing at the expression on his face, she hurried off towards the house, and, looking back at Robbie, and not where she was going, she ran straight into Sir Peter Grenville's arms.

'Well, well, now!' he exclaimed, a sardonic look on his still handsome, but definitely debauched face. 'And what has the little, prim secretary miss been doing with the chauffeur, eh?'

As he spoke, Sir Peter still kept Kate imprisoned in his arms.

'Sir, I would thank you to let me go!'

Kate exclaimed indignantly.

Sir Peter laughed and it wasn't a pleasant sound.

'And if it doesn't please me to do so?'

'Then you are no gentleman, sir!'

'A right little vixen, aren't you?' he said, pulling her even closer to him, and then his mouth had come crashing down on hers, with savage, bruising force. Kate squirmed and twisted in his arms, genuinely frightened now. Why, surely the man must be out of his mind.

Somehow, fear lending her strength, Kate managed to kick her employer on the shin, and he loosened his grip on her, at the same time emitting a sound which could have been pain — or anger, probably a mixture of both.

'Why, you she devil!'

Even his words were cut off as Kate lifted her hand and slapped him across his impudent face, before running around to the back of the house where she entered by the servants' and tradespeople's entrance.

'What's the matter with you?' Nellie Faragher asked.

She was assistant cook and currently in charge as Gaston had had to return to France because his mother was very seriously ill. Kate knew that she must look a sorry sight, wet, bedraggled and both angry and frightened after her singularly unpleasant encounter with Sir Peter Grenville.

'I was silly enough to go out without a coat and got pretty wet. It's quite a tidy walk from the secretarial school to here.'

'That's as may be,' Nellie observed shrewdly, 'but you look as if you've had a fright to me.'

Kate's cheeks were flushed, her eyes wide and wild looking.

'Has Sir Peter been botherin' you?' she asked bluntly.

'No,' Kate began, and then, seeing the sympathy in the older woman's eyes, she sank down on a chair at the kitchen table. 'Yes,' she said.

'Well, I can't say that I'm surprised!

You're a right beauty, that you are, and His Lordship, well, he's an eye for the women, so he has. I reckon that's why he's took you on in the first place.'

'Oh, Nellie, what will I do? I was a bit worried about him, but I thought things would be all right when his wife came. But instead, well, he was worse today.'

'Speak to young Mr Roger. He's a good, decent chap, not a bit like his father. He'll advise you as to what you can do about it.'

'Oh, Nellie, I couldn't! I'd be too embarrassed!'

'Then you're a fool, girl, and I hadn't taken you for one, either! What choice have you got. Leave a soft job, give up your schoolin' and go into one of them fish factories or the like?'

Kate bit her lip. She suddenly felt that everything was hopeless. She didn't want to go into a factory, but how could she avoid him, when he was her employer, when she had to work with him?

At that moment, the kitchen door,

which Kate had left ajar, burst open unceremoniously, and Roger Grenville stood there, his face pale with anger.

'Is what I've just heard true?' he asked, his voice scarcely more than a whisper, and yet, somehow, all the more deadly for being so.

'Yes,' Nellie said bluntly to Roger, before Kate could say anything.

'But he's disgusting!' Roger exclaimed and crossed the room in a few long strides to put a comforting arm about Kate's shoulders. 'I'm so terribly sorry, my dear! But don't worry about it, I'll sort it out.'

Then, just as quickly as he had arrived, Roger left.

'Oh, Nellie, what's going to happen now?'

Nellie's face was grim as she replied.

'Things'll get better, you'll see! That Sir Peter, he won't want no scandal, not with him trying to get that government contract to open a munitions' factory, and his wife just arrived, too.'

'I hope you're right,' Kate said, but

even to her own ears, her voice sounded uncertain.

It seemed, though, that whatever Roger had said to his father had been successful, for Sir Peter was coldly polite when he summoned Kate and gave her some letters to type for him. It was as if nothing untoward had occurred between them, and Kate could only hope and pray that things would continue that way.

Robbie was permitted to use the car the following evening, and his and Kate's trip to the Odeon went ahead as planned. Robbie, however, seemed a bit edgy. Kate soon found out why.

'Did I see His Lordship stop you just as I was turning the car yesterday?' he asked as he gave her a packet of sweets to enjoy during the film.

'Yes,' Kate said briefly.

'What did he want?' Robbie persisted. 'He seemed to be trying to detain you like. He wasn't bothering you, was he?'

'He was making a bit of a nuisance of

himself,' Kate admitted, and stealing a glance at Robbie's irate expression, was sorry that she'd done so. 'But it's all sorted out now, nothing at all to worry about,' she added hastily.

'That man is a good-for-nothing lecher!' Robbie said angrily.

'He's probably just typical of his class.'

'A bad example, I would say! Well, don't you go standing for no nonsense from the likes of him! Just let me know if he's bothering you, and I'll speak to my dad and mum. There'd be room for you to stay at the farm with them, and you could help Mum out a bit. You wouldn't earn much, but you'd have a roof over your head and could keep going to your classes.'

Kate was touched by his obvious sincerity.

'That's very kind of you, Robbie, and I promise that I'll keep your offer in mind, but I'm sure it won't come to that.'

Kate certainly hoped that it wouldn't,

for if she took up Robbie's offer, it would be akin to saying that she would marry him, and although she liked him, she didn't love him. She smiled wryly. No, poor fool that she was, she very much suspected that she was falling in love with the obnoxious Sir Peter's son, and there could never be any future in that, so she would do well to get such foolish notions out of her fanciful head.

Robbie and Kate continued to go out together about twice a week. Robbie wanted Kate to agree to get engaged to him, pointing out that there was a very real chance of war, and he wanted there to be a commitment between them. But Kate continued to prevaricate, ostensibly because she was working hard for the exams she would take in July, but also because she couldn't help how she felt about Roger Grenville.

It wasn't that she saw that much of Roger, although, with the better weather which had at last come to the island, he had taken to asking her to ride with him, something which he had taught her, for she had had very little experience of horse-riding, other than to canter round one of the local farmers fields when she was a youngster. They also walked Roger's dog, a lively black spaniel called Bess, and sometimes took a picnic lunch with them. But they were always somewhere quiet, out in the country, and Kate, although she knew that Roger wasn't a snob, still couldn't help but feel that he was ashamed to be seen with her in public.

Perhaps that wasn't entirely fair, perhaps ashamed wasn't quite the right word. Islanders were gossips and it wouldn't do for the master of The Grange's son to be seen with the former gardener's daughter. Nevertheless, it still irritated Kate a bit, made her feel insecure, so she was surprised, but very pleased, by Roger's reaction, when, out for a morning's ride, she told him that her father had asked her to call and see him, for he had some good news to tell her.

'Did he say what it is?' Roger asked.

'No.' Kate shook her head. 'As you know, I've been to see him a few times at the farm now, but this message came through Robbie.'

Roger's lips tightened slightly. So she was still seeing his father's chauffeur. He wasn't really too surprised, and yet he couldn't help but hope that the situation between them wasn't too serious.

'Kate, I don't know how your father will feel about seeing me, but do you think, rather, would you mind, if I came with you when you go to see him?'

'Roger, are you sure?'

This was it! He did care about her, otherwise he surely wouldn't have made such a suggestion. Roger misinterpreted her reaction, thinking there was too much ill-will. Although she had shown him friendship, Kate still resented him because of his father. He gave a bitter laugh.

'I would like to come, but perhaps it isn't such a good idea after all.'

So he did feel that she was beneath

him. Kate was hurt, and couldn't keep a hurt note out of her voice as she said, 'It probably isn't, given the fact that you're gentry and I'm just a working man's daughter!'

'Kate, that isn't what I meant at all!' Roger protested hotly. 'I just didn't want to embarrass you. I wasn't thinking of my feelings, I assure you! Speaking for myself, I would love to meet your father and your whole family, come to that.'

He dismounted, then pulled her gently down from her mount. Then, before Kate was aware of what he intended, Roger's arms were around her, and he was hugging her to him.

'Oh, Kate! Don't you know yet how I feel about you?'

Kate disengaged herself from his embrace, and looked up at him sadly.

'I hoped that you cared,' she admitted.

'Then you care about me, too?'

'Yes.'

The one word was drawn from her

reluctantly, for what future could there be for them?

'Oh, my darling, that's wonderful! I'll come with you and tell your father how we feel about each other, and . . . '

Kate shook her head sadly.

'Much as I would like that, Roger, can't you see that it's impossible? What future can you have with me, a former gardener's daughter?'

'I've been thinking about this,' he admitted, 'and the world is changing. Fortunately, the old, pompous, snobbish values are dying. I'm still not convinced that there's going to be a war, but I do admit that there could be. But whether there is or not, life really hasn't been the same since the Great War. Values changed after that, only people like my father, entrenched as he is in the old ways, is too blind to accept it.'

'And he certainly wouldn't accept me. Why, he even saw me as a light of love. I think he half intended to exercise his rights of ownership, which must surely have died out hundreds of years ago!'

'Kate, I'm over twenty-one! I don't intend to be dictated to by a father whom I certainly don't admire, and, if I'm to be perfectly truthful, don't even like over much! No, you must let me come with you to see your father. You owe me the right to make his acquaintance, to let him judge me for myself, rather than thinking me just like my father.'

Kate sighed.

'All right, if you definitely want to come with me, then do, but I can't be sure what kind of reception you'll get from my father, at least not at first. For all that he's poor, he's a very proud man, and he was very hurt, and angry, with your father's treatment of him.'

'Kate, I understand and sympathise with him. I want the opportunity of meeting him so that I can show him that my father and I are as different as chalk and cheese.'

The meeting between Walter Christian and Roger Grenville went off far better than Kate had believed possible. Why, the two men actually seemed to like one another! At first, of course, things had been a bit stilted, but the fact that Roger was so obviously a very different kettle of fish from his father had soon become apparent to the astute Walter Christian. And, besides, Walter had every reason to be happy. Farmer Kelly, realising that he was an excellent worker, had recently announced that Walter would be promoted to farm manager. The promotion included a cottage, which meant that Margaret and the girls would be able to move in in a few days' time.

Kate, of course, had had to confess her deception to her father, that she was working as a part-time secretary up at The Grange, and living in. There had been no banker's daughter friend by the name of Cathy. Walter had looked as if he was annoyed, but then he had seen the funny side of it.

'Well, one thing I will grant you, lass, and that's that you're a right canny one! You had us well and truly taken in!'

Kate had had the grace to look embarrassed.

'I am sorry, Dad, truly I am. But if I had told you the truth, well, you wouldn't have allowed me to do it, would you? And you see, it really has been for the best.'

'Aye, well, what your mother will have to say about it, I don't know.'

Kate looked worried. She didn't want to upset her mother, who had been through quite enough. Walter took pity on her.

'Don't fret, Katie. Your mother will be so pleased to have a place of our own again that she won't take it too badly. Leastways not when she knows that things are working out well for you.'

'I'll come and see you all in a few days, once you've had time to settle in,' Kate assured her father as she and Roger prepared to leave.

'Aye, make sure you do, an' all,' he said, then he grinned at Roger. 'And you can come along with her, too, young man, if you like. I know Margaret, my wife, will make you very welcome.'

'Thank you, sir, I'd be pleased to.'

The two men shook hands, and then Roger helped Kate on to her horse, and they made their way back to The Grange, well satisfied with their visit to Walter Christian.

Kate slept better that night. Oh, she still had problems, no doubt about it, but her father's acceptance of Roger had cheered her spirits, and she was beginning to wonder if perhaps there could be a future for them after all.

But perhaps she was being unrealistic. Sir Peter would be horrified, and for all that Lady Alicia was pleasant to her, Kate couldn't really believe that the aristocratic lady would want a gardener's daughter as her daughter-in-law. Still, she wasn't going to worry about it now, not when she had to take her exams in a few days' time. They were important and she must keep her mind clear at least until she got them over with.

Kate was deeply entrenched in a dream where she had passed all her exams with flying colours, and Lady Alicia and Sir Peter were telling her how clever she was and how proud they'd be to have her as their daughter-in-law, when she suddenly became aware of the acrid smell of smoke in her nostrils. She always slept with at least one window open, even in winter. Now, still slightly groggy from sleep, she scrambled out of bed and over to the window.

The night was alight with a rich orange glow. Kate frowned, and then realisation dawned. It was a fire, and, if she wasn't very much mistaken, it was coming from the direction of the stables!

7

Kate didn't stop to get dressed. She pulled on her dressing-gown over her long nightdress and pushed her feet into a pair of walking shoes. It was a windy night, but dry, which meant that the fire would spread all the more quickly.

Lady Alicia was just coming out of her bedroom as Kate dashed along the corridor. Sir Peter and his wife had a room together for appearance's sake, which they occasionally used, but Lady Alicia preferred to use her own room, and Kate honestly couldn't say that she blamed her!

'What is it? What is going on?'

'I think there's a fire in the stables, Lady Alicia. I'm going to find out.'

She made to dash past the older lady, but Lady Alicia caught her arm.

'I will go and ring for the fire brigade

to come, but there is no point in going out there, my dear. Leave it to the men. This isn't women's work!'

'Call the fire brigade, by all means, but I must see what's happening!'

Kate pulled herself free and dashed down the staircase.

Once outside, the acrid smell of burning hit Kate with staggering force. She had been right — it was coming from the stables, where the mare, Winsome, was housed, the mare which Roger Grenville had taught her to ride. Horses were screaming with fright. Somehow she must save them.

'Kate, stop!' a voice shouted, and strong arms reached out and grasped hold of her as she made to enter the blazing stables.

It was Robbie Karran. Kate struggled in his arms.

'Don't be so foolish! There's nothing you can do!' he persuaded her.

But Kate wasn't thinking rationally, especially when he added, 'Sir Peter and his son are in there, and I'm sure the fire brigade will be here soon.'

But Kate was no longer listening to him. She was twisting and turning frantically in his arms. When this didn't work, sheer instinct took over, and she kicked him on the shin. Involuntarily, his hold on Kate loosened, and she broke free.

'Kate, come back!' he shouted, but his voice was carried away by the freshening wind.

It was a nightmare inside the stables. Kate was coughing, choking, spluttering, but the mare, Winsome, had somehow managed to break free from her stall and, eyes wild with terror, was charging towards her.

'Winsome!' Kate cried, lunging for the mare's bridle. 'Here, girl.'

But Winsome, maddened by fear, charged straight at Kate, knocking her off her feet. Kate fell heavily, hitting her head and temporarily losing consciousness. She was still decidedly muzzy when someone leaned over her, gently scooped her up in his arms and murmured, 'Oh, Kate, my darling! You could have been killed.'

'Roger,' she whispered, and then snuggled into his comforting arms.

Winsome had managed to escape from the blazing stables, but Roger's mount, Nero, was still inside. Roger was concerned about Kate, who still seemed to be only semi-conscious, but he was also very worried at the prospect of his horse dying in the blaze. Robbie was hovering at the edge of the stables when Roger, carrying Kate, came out.

'Look after her for me,' he said. 'I've got to get Nero out of there.'

With that, he thrust Kate into Robbie's willing arms.

'Roger, what . . . ' she muttered, but her voice still wasn't very coherent.

Roger threw her an anguished look, and then dashed back into the stables, where the fire was now fiercer, fanned by the increasing wind.

'It's all right, Kate, the fire brigade will be here any moment now, and the horse you've been riding is safe. So I'll take you back to the house and get you a brandy. It will do you good. You've had a very nasty shock.'

'But Roger's gone back in there! He could be killed! I must go back and help him!'

'He won't die. His sort isn't that easy to get rid of!' Robbie muttered.

It wasn't that he had anything against Roger Grenville personally, it was just that they loved the same woman!

He entrusted Kate to Nellie Faragher, the cook.

'Come on, my lady, a strong, medicinal brandy is the best thing for you!'

Kate didn't argue. Although she didn't care much for the taste of brandy, she did feel as if she needed something to revive her.

'Thank you,' she said demurely, as the glass was put in her hand.

She swallowed it dutifully, and had to admit that the liquor stopped her trembling so much, and put a warm feeling in her stomach.

'That's enough,' she said, getting to her feet. 'Now I think I'd like to go to my room and rest.'

Robbie immediately stood up.

'I'll escort you.'

'There's no need,' Kate replied, with a chill smile.

She actually had no intention of going to her room. She was going back outside to find out how Roger was, and Robbie Karran wasn't going to stand in her way! Cook hid a smile. She guessed what Kate was up to and, if that was the way the land lay, then good luck to her!

'Robbie, you and I can take a dram together. Kate's looking fine now. There's no need for you to be seeing her to her room. It's the middle of the night. The poor wee thing would do better to be getting her rest! You can have a nightcap with me, and then, if we're not needed any more, we'll both gladly take ourselves off to our beds.'

When Kate went back outside, she could see, even from a distance, that the fire brigade had arrived and the fire was now under control. The horses' cries had subsided into whimpers. She was actually outside the stables, now smouldering rather than blazing. Firemen seemed to be everywhere. She spoke to one.

'Is Mr Roger Grenville all right?'

'Reckon he's still in there,' he said. 'Sir Peter was brought out and is on his way to hospital with burns to his hands. Reckon he was trying to save his face and . . . '

He got no further, for Kate had run into the stables.

'Hey! You can't go in there!' he shouted after her.

But Kate had already gone. She met two firemen carrying Roger out on a stretcher, masks over their faces.

'How is he?' she asked, her voice trembling.

'He's got burns,' he said, then seeing the poignant anguish on her lovely face, he softened, and patting her shoulder, added, 'but he'll live.'

An ambulance was waiting for Roger

and, he, too, was taken to hospital. Kate longed to go with him but, of course, that was quite impossible. Even the feckless Lady Alicia had appeared on the scene by this time and it was she who accompanied him to the hospital. Kate, not knowing how badly injured Roger was, went back to the house feeling miserable and with a headache, a combination of her fall, the brandy, lack of sleep and worry.

If she had been able to reach her room without interference, it might have been better but, instead, she met Robbie as soon as she entered the house. Having had a very generous nightcap with Nellie, he was now inclined to be belligerent.

'Where the devil do you think you've been, eh? Oh, don't tell me, I know! Looking for young Mr Roger, eh? Well, miss, let me tell you now, and tell you good, I overheard the mistress talking with young Nellie Brook, her personal maid. There's a Miss Veronica Hill-Stevens coming over here soon. She's the daughter of her ladyship's best friend, a Lady Westwood, apparently, and her ladyship, well, she's hoping that young Roger and this Miss Hill-Stevens are going to make a go of it, so to speak.'

Kate was exasperated.

'Oh, just shut up, Robbie, will you!'

She flounced off up the stairs, leaving him standing there open-mouthed.

'I'll join the Reservists, so I will!' Robbie shouted after Kate, once he'd got his breath back. 'There's going to be a war, young lady, you mark my words, and Robbie Karran is no coward. He'll be one of the first in line!'

Kate turned, gave him a withering look, and said, 'Oh, yes, I noticed that you were first in line when it came to saving the horses!'

'Kate, wait!' he called after her. 'You must see that you're not for the likes of him. He's gentry, whereas you're working-class, like me. We've got a future together, Kate. Don't spoil it!'

'Robbie, I'm going to bed,' she called

back over her shoulder, 'and I suggest you do the same!'

Then, not waiting to see whether he was still there or not, she hurried up the remaining stairs and along the corridor to her room. She didn't think he'd come after her, but she locked the door nonetheless.

Despite being dog-tired, Kate couldn't get off to sleep and, sighing with exasperation, picked up her shorthand notes, but she couldn't concentrate on them, either, despite the fact that she was due to sit both her shorthand and typewriting exams in two days' time. Well, that depended on Roger's condition now. If he was too seriously ill, she would just have to put them off, no matter what her parents or the principal of the college thought. They would think her an absolute fool, and perhaps she was. She laughed mirthlessly. She was in love with Roger and she knew he cared for her, although, in her heart of hearts, she suspected that Robbie was right, and that there could be no future for them.

She eventually fell into a troubled sleep.

Kate woke up feeling tired and groggy, sunlight streaming into the bedroom. She looked at the clock on the bedside cabinet. It was after ten o'clock. With an exclamation of horror, Kate leaped out of bed and pulled on her clothes. How could she have fallen asleep when Roger's very life might well be in danger? Then, as she hurriedly dragged a hairbrush through her tangled hair, she smiled grimly at her reflection. Her face was pale with dark shadows under her eyes, evidence of lack of sleep.

Kate hurried out of the room and downstairs to the kitchen where Nellie would surely know what was going on.

'Oh, love, how are you feeling?' Nellie greeted her. 'I was just wondering if I should send Violet up to see if you were all right, but then I thought, if she's asleep, then let her stay that way. After all, it was precious little sleep you had last night.'

'No-one had much sleep, Nellie, but you're up and about your work. I should have been, too.'

'Nonsense, girl, I . . . '

But Kate interrupted her.

'How is he? There must be some news!'

'I take it you're talking about young Mr Roger and not the other one,' Nellie replied wryly. 'Sir Peter is scarcely hurt at all, and was discharged from the hospital immediately a doctor had looked at him. He's resting in his room now. Her ladyship had a bed made up for herself at the hospital and stayed overnight with Mr Roger. In fact, she's still there and there's been no word from her, so we don't know how he is.'

Kate was horrified.

'But has no-one thought to telephone the hospital and ask about him?'

'That snotty-nosed fellow, Worthington, the butler, probably has, but he certainly hasn't seen fit to confide in me!'

'Then I'll go and ask him right away,' Kate said, turning towards the door, then she changed her mind. 'On second thoughts, it's probably better if I ring the hospital direct.'

So saying, she hurried to Sir Peter's study and, finding the door unlocked, went in and telephoned the hospital. When she explained that she was Sir Peter's secretary she had no trouble at all.

'He's in a private room in the private wing,' the woman said, 'and his condition is stable. He suffered some burns to his hands and face, but they certainly aren't critical. Of course, he's had a nasty shock and when he recovered consciousness, he was in considerable pain. But he has been given an injection and is sleeping peacefully now.'

'When will I be able to see him?'

Kate couldn't keep the anxiety out of her voice, but the nurse hesitated.

141

'That's a difficult one to answer, I'm afraid. He's been given something to make him sleep, which really is the best cure for him at the moment.'

'Yes, yes, I can appreciate that. But I really would like to see him!'

The nurse realised that Sir Peter Grenville's secretary was showing an unusual interest in his son. Her kind heart was touched, but there was nothing she could do. Dr Atkinson had been adamant that the young man would only be able to see family for the time being and even then, the visits were to be kept short, so that he didn't become over-tired. She explained the situation to Kate as gently as she could and Kate, realising that there was nothing more she could do for now, was forced to accept it.

Lady Grenville returned to The Grange shortly before lunch and Kate, who should have been getting ready to go to secretarial school to prepare for her exams asked if she might speak to her. Fortunately for Kate, her request was granted and she was soon in Alicia's bedroom. Her ladyship looked tired, although almost as immaculately turned out as usual. She smiled at Kate, but the latter fancied that there was a slight coldness in her eyes.

'Kate, I'm pleased to see you, of course,' she said, not sounding as if she meant it. 'But as you will appreciate, it has been a very long and stressful time for me recently. Now I want to rest, so whatever it is that you wish to say, will you kindly keep it brief?'

'I want to visit your son,' she said without preamble.

Lady Alicia's eyebrows rose.

'Really, my dear, that is most kind of you, but quite impossible! I'm afraid that Roger, Mr Roger, is only able to see family at the present time and you most definitely aren't that, my dear!'

Lady Alicia then turned away.

'How is he, Lady Alicia?' Kate asked, addressing the lady's back.

Lady Alicia spun round, her dark eyes glittering dangerously.

'He suffered burns to his face. Of course, it is bandaged at present, but we do not yet know if there will be any scarring. There, now are you satisfied? Now, will you kindly leave?'

And Lady Alicia walked over to the window and stared out. Kate knew then this seemingly shallow woman was actually very upset.

'Thank you, Lady Alicia,' she said gently, and left the room, closing the door quietly behind her.

8

Kate didn't want to take her exams that Friday but she knew that she must. Not to do so wouldn't have been fair to her parents or Mrs Rogers, all of whom had been so good to her.

That morning, Robbie had presented her with a bunch of lovely carnations and had shamefacedly apologised for his behaviour on the night of the fire. Kate instantly forgave him. She had been very cross at the time, but realised that it was only because he'd had too much to drink.

'May I take you to the school and pick you up afterwards?' he asked.

Kate couldn't help but smile.

'Really, Robbie, there's no need. It's a nice day and the walk will be good for me. Anyway, won't Sir Peter need you?'

'No. There's a couple of fellows from the government coming here to talk to him about the munitions' factory, so he won't need the car for a while.'

Kate would just have soon walked, but Robbie was so keen that she didn't like hurting his feelings.

'OK, then, if that's what you want to do,' she said, a little ungraciously.

Robbie didn't even notice.

Despite the fact that she was worried about Roger, Kate knew that her exams, typewriting and shorthand, went well.

'You won't have the results until the start of next month,' Mrs Rogers told her afterwards, 'but you've never had any problems with the others, so I'm sure that you'll pass your finals with flying colours.'

'I hope so, ma'am.'

Kate looked momentarily anxious. Mrs Rogers took pity on her.

'I'll have a look at them before I send them off to Liverpool,' she offered. 'I should have a good idea.'

'Oh, would you? That would be wonderful!'

'No problem at all,' Mr Rogers replied, smiling. 'Technically, you've finished your studies here now, Kate, but call in whenever you get the time and I'll let you know. Anyway, I'd like to keep in touch with you.'

Kate's eyes misted with tears.

'Thank you for being so kind to me.'

'It's been a pleasure, dear. As I told your employer, Sir Peter, you're the most gifted student whom I've had the pleasure to teach.'

Robbie was sitting outside in the Bentley. He got out and opened the passenger door for Kate. Seeing that she was smiling, he smiled, too.

'I take it that you've done OK.'

'I think so,' Kate replied, going on to say that the principal was going to check her exam papers and let her know if she thought Kate had passed.

'You're sure to have done,' Robbie replied positively. 'And there's other news, too. Sir Peter has been given permission to open his factory and is

147

discussing alterations to Simpson's kipper works.'

Kate raised her eyebrows.

'But what's the kipper factory got to do with it?'

'Apparently the old blighter, sure that he'd get his own way in the end, had already bought the factory. I gather he'd agreed to keep on anyone who wants to work in munitions, otherwise he'll bring in new people from the mainland.'

'Well, I suppose he can't do anything else,' Kate replied, striving to be fair. 'At least they've got the chance, which was more than poor Dad!'

'Aye, well, they're mainly young ones. I was going to suggest taking you out for tea again. I'd have liked that, but Sir Peter wants me to drive him to the factory, so I'm afraid we'll have to go straight back to the house.'

He leaned across and gave one of her hands a gentle squeeze.

'I'm really sorry, Kate. I'd intended it to be a bit of a treat, and by way of apology, like, for my behaviour the other night. Reckon I'm going to be kept busy these next few days, running his lordship back and forth to the factory and collecting that young lady, that Miss Hill-Stevens, from the boat.'

Kate's face paled.

'When is she arriving?' she asked.

Robbie, still brooding about the fact that he probably wouldn't have much time to see Kate, failed to notice her concern.

'On the afternoon boat tomorrow. She'll be in about six o'clock.'

'I see. When did this arrangement come about?'

'I don't know for sure, but Nellie reckoned that Lady Alicia phoned the young lady's mother, Lady Westwood, to tell her about Mr Roger's accident. Well, I suppose Miss Hill-Stevens was upset and wanted to come and see for herself how he's faring.'

'Yes, I suppose she would do,' Kate said, biting her bottom lip to stop its slight tremble.

Then a thought occurred to her. Miss Hill-Stevens wasn't family, even if she was gentry and a family friend, which meant that the rule of family-only visits to Roger must have been relaxed.

Just to be sure, Kate rang the hospital once alone back at The Grange, and was told that Roger Grenville was now able to receive visitors.

'Whom shall I tell him is calling?' the nurse asked.

Kate hesitated, then said, 'Don't say anything. I'd rather keep it a surprise.'

* * *

Kate gave her name to the woman sitting behind the reception desk in the hospital's private wing and asked to see Mr Roger Grenville.

'Are you a friend of the family?' she asked.

'I'm Sir Peter's secretary,' Kate replied.

'Oh, I see. Well, that should be in

order. Do you want one of the nurses to take you there?'

'No, thank you,' Kate replied, already moving away.

She found the room easily and after tapping lightly on the door, pushed it open. Roger was sitting up in bed, a book in one hand. The other hand, she quickly saw, was bandaged. He looked up, startled. Clearly, he hadn't heard her soft knock. The book fell from his hand.

'Kate, no! You shouldn't have come here!' he said, his voice anguished, and Kate saw that whilst one side of his face was perfect, the other had an ugly red mark running from the bottom of his left eye down to the corner of his mouth. 'Go away! I don't want you here!' he cried, half-turning away from her so that the injured side of his face was no longer visible.

Kate ran over to the bed and took his uninjured hand in hers.

'Roger, don't be silly! As if a little thing like that would matter to me!

How are you feeling? That's much more important.'

But he kept his face averted from her as he said, 'I'll live! But I'm not ready for visitors, Kate. I'm surprised the hospital let you in to see me.'

Kate was stung by his coldness. She put her small gift for him, some grapes, on the cabinet by his bed, as she tried to compose herself. Even so, her voice wasn't quite steady as she spoke.

'But I had to come, Roger! I've been so worried about you!'

'Well, now you know that there's no reason for you to be, you can go back home.'

He laughed, a bitter, hollow sound.

'Actually, I'm amazed that you've got the time to visit me. I would have thought that father would be keeping you very busy now that he's got his heart's desire, his munitions' factory.'

'Actually he doesn't need me right now. He's too busy supervising the alterations to be interested in mundane things like secretarial work.'

'I wasn't referring to your secretarial skills, my dear,' Roger drawled, in a voice which was entirely at odds with his usual kindly tone. 'No, I was thinking more of your other attributes. He finds you very attractive, and dear Father has always had a weakness for the fair sex!'

He was being unreasonably yet deliberately insulting, and they both knew it. Kate sucked in her breath to stop herself from retorting angrily.

'I'll pretend you haven't just said that,' she forced herself to say calmly. 'You've had a horrible experience, and I think that the memories are still affecting your logic. But you must try to put all that out of your mind and get strong and well.'

His harsh laugh interrupted her.

'What for? So that Father can stick me in his munitions' factory? Or maybe one of the Services will take on a scarred wreck of a man with a damaged left hand!'

'Roger, you're depressed. I can

sympathise with that but things will get better every day. Its very early days yet.'

He put his good hand to his forehead and rubbed it across.

'Kate, are you going to go away and leave me in peace because you're giving me a headache, or do I have to ring the bell and summon help to have you thrown out?'

Kate recoiled from the pure ice in his voice. He meant it! Her legs felt like jelly and all she wanted to do was sink into the nearest chair and burst into tears for a love which was surely irretrievably shattered, a love which had seemed so real, despite their different stations in life. Although his face was half-averted, he could still see her. He sighed.

'Well, what are you going to do? I mean it, you know!'

And to illustrate the point, his good hand began to move in the direction of the bell which would summon one of the nursing staff.

'All right, I'm going. Take care,

Roger, and try to get better and rid yourself of such bitterness.'

Then, stifling a sob with difficulty, she ran from the room. Once outside the door, Kate took a handkerchief from her coat pocket and dabbed at her eyes as she rushed from the building. She might have felt better if she had known that inside his hospital room, a solitary tear was sliding down Roger Grenville's unblemished cheek.

The next day, Sir Peter kept Kate busy with mundane duties such as ordering supplies for his factory, which he planned to open the following week. After telling her what he wanted her to do, he left Kate to it. She was glad, although she doubted that Sir Peter would have been much of a threat to her at present. For once, munitions were paramount in his mind.

Later on in the day, Lady Grenville asked to see Kate, and when she went to Alicia's room, she was asked to go with Robbie to meet Veronica Hill-Stevens off the boat.

'I had intended to go myself,' Lady Alicia said, 'but my son is not in good spirits and I feel that he needs me more than Miss Hill-Stevens. I know that this isn't really in your line of duty, Kate, but it doesn't seem quite the thing to entrust Veronica to my husband's chauffeur.'

'I'm sure Robbie would act impeccably,' Kate replied.

'I know he would, and I don't mean anything like that!' Alicia smiled. 'No, I'm really excusing myself. My friend, Lady Westwood, will expect me to meet her daughter, which I would definitely do under normal circumstances. But, to be honest, Kate, I'm worried about my son's state of mind at the moment. The accident has disturbed him. You and Veronica are of a similar age. She will be pleased to see you.'

Kate didn't feel at all sure about that, but there was nothing she could do, for although Lady Alicia had phrased it very politely, she wasn't really asking Kate to go, she was telling her to.

'I'll be pleased to go with Robbie,' Kate said, and even meant it, if Roger's mother could do anything to help bring Roger back to normal.

Robbie was thrilled that Kate was going with him and gave her a light kiss on the cheek before putting the Bentley into gear and pulling away from The Grange.

'Do you know, I was thinking that I wouldn't get to see you for days with Sir Peter keeping me on the go, and now I'm seeing you the very next day!'

He grinned and raised his eyes heavenwards.

'Somebody up there must be thinking about me after all!'

Kate laughed. Robbie could be very good company and she was genuinely fond of him. He would make a good husband for someone, and he was of her own class. Her lips twisted wryly. If only she could get Roger Grenville out of her mind.

'You know, I am a bit of a dolt,' Robbie was saying now. 'I'd quite forgotten that it's Sunday tomorrow and I get Sundays off anyway, munitions factory or not. Why don't you come and have dinner with us at the farm? I know my mum and dad would love to meet you.'

Kate hesitated, and then thought, why not? Roger's dismissal of her at the hospital had been very brutal and had hurt her a lot. It was probably due to the shock and pain of his injuries, but then again, perhaps there was more to it than that. Perhaps he thought of her as an embarrassment now that the eminently suitable Veronica Hill-Stevens would shortly be arriving on the scene.

Mind made up, Kate said, 'That's very nice of you, Robbie. If you're sure that your parents won't mind?'

Robbie looked incredulous and then delighted.

'Mind? They'll be over the moon!'

The Snaefell had docked early and when Robbie parked the car and they walked to where she was berthed, they could see a beautifully-dressed young lady pacing restlessly up and down the quayside.

'Miss Hill-Stevens?' Kate asked, tapping her on the shoulder.

Veronica spun round and Kate saw that she had luxuriant blonde curls on which a little navy pillar box hat sat provocatively. She was very pretty but the petulant set of her cupid's mouth wasn't so endearing and neither were her dark eyes, which were presently snapping with temper.

'Who are you?' she demanded, her voice loud and arrogant, the tone rude. 'Where is my godmother, Lady Grenville? I've been off that wretched boat for almost half an hour and it's positively freezing waiting round here!'

That was a definite exaggeration as by island standards, the evening was pleasantly warm.

'Lady Alicia sends her apologies.' Kate hoped her voice sounded soothing.

'But she's had to go to the hospital to see her son. He's rather depressed after the incident in the barn.'

She beckoned to Robbie, who stepped forward, lifted his cloth cap and made the young lady a slight bow. He looked very uneasy.

'This young man is Robbie Karran, Sir Peter's chauffeur, and I am his secretary, Kate Christian.'

Miss Hill-Stevens looked at them from head to toe in a way that suggested that she found them loathsome insects who had dared to crawl out of the undergrowth!

'Aunt Alicia has entrusted me to you?'

The tone was incredulous, and Kate found that her hand was itching to smack the spoiled beauty on one of her powdered cheeks. Of course, wisdom prevailed, and she did no such thing.

'It's only a short distance to The Grange,' she said, 'where Nellie, who is acting as cook at the moment, has prepared a special dinner for you.'

Veronica wasn't impressed by this information.

'But Mother told me Aunt Alicia had a French chef!'

'Gaston had to return to Paris to look after his sick mother,' Kate replied. 'But you won't be disappointed. Nellie is an excellent cook. Now, as you are so cold, you'd no doubt like to make your way to the car.'

She pointed to the Bentley, parked as near as possible to the adjacent carpark. Veronica glared at Robbie.

'Can't you bring it any nearer?' she demanded, her voice petulant.

'I'm truly sorry, miss, but I've brought it as near as I can,' Robbie mumbled, his eyes not meeting hers.

'Oh, very well then!' she said and then strode off ahead of them.

It was an uncomfortable journey back, as Kate's attempts at conversation were greeted with monosyllabic replies from Veronica, which made the time seem longer than it actually was. At last, though, they were there, and Sir Peter had actually torn himself away from his factory to dine with his new guest. He had invited Kate to join them but one look at Veronica's face told her she wasn't welcome and she said that she would have her meal in her room. Sir Peter looked amused. He had seen the look the snobbish Miss Hill-Stevens had bestowed on Kate.

'All right, but I'll expect you to dine with us in future, Kate.'

'As you wish, Sir Peter.'

Kate inclined her head and then made an excuse and hurried off to the kitchen where she intended to have her meal with Robbie and Nellie.

'Spoiled piece, is she?'

Nellie smiled at Kate as she put a plate with chicken, new potatoes and an assortment of vegetables in front of her.

'Very spoiled,' Kate said, scowling at the memory of Veronica's arrogant expression. 'Thanks, Nellie, this is really sumptuous.'

'Yes, you're a mighty good cook, Nellie,' Robbie agreed.

He gave Kate a gentle nudge.

'Mind you, my mum can do just as well!'

He saw Nellie's expression, and quickly added, 'Well, it might be a bit plainer, like, but still very fine. It'll be roast beef and spuds tomorrow, with all the trimmings, of course!'

Their evening together was cut short as Robbie had to go to the hospital to bring Lady Grenville home. Sir Peter went with Robbie to pay a short visit to his son and Kate was detailed to take care of Veronica, a task which she didn't relish. Veronica had retired to her room, but Kate felt that she'd go and see if there was anything she wanted.

'Oh, it's you,' Veronica greeted Kate ungraciously. 'What do you want?'

'I don't want anything, but Sir Peter asked me to check to see if you do.'

Veronica's eyes narrowed.

'Oh, yes, you're his secretary, aren't you?' she said with an insulting emphasis on the word, secretary.

'Yes, I am.'

'And no doubt you're also paid for

— shall we say, other services?'

There was no mistaking her meaning and Kate coloured. What an unpleasant and impudent young woman Veronica was!

'I'm paid to do book-keeping as well,' Kate said, holding on to her temper with difficulty. 'Now, Miss Hill-Stevens, is there anything I can do for you or would you prefer me to leave you alone so that you can rest?'

Veronica's eyes twinkled wickedly.

'Why ever should I wish to rest? I'm not some old fogey who needs to be in bed by nine o'clock! You may sit there.'

She indicated a hard-backed, un-comfortable-looking chair. Kate's lips tightened, but she had no option but to sit down.

'I suppose I should really have gone with Uncle Peter to see Mr Roger,' Veronica said, talking more to herself than to Kate. 'But I don't wish to appear too eager and, well, what am I going to find? Was he badly injured in the fire? There's going to be a war, you know, and although I do love Roger to pieces, I just couldn't stand being cooped up here, far away from town!'

Her eyes narrowed, and she looked hard and calculating.

'Tell me, is he service material?' she asked.

Kate shook her head.

'That's something I can't answer. You'll have to speak to Lady Alicia.'

Her tone was cold as she was finding that she disliked Veronica Hill-Stevens more and more each minute.

'Oh, haven't you seen him, then?'

She didn't give Kate time to answer, so Kate was saved from having to lie to her, for she had no intention of telling Veronica that she had done so.

'No, well, you won't have, not being family! Mr Roger and I have been expected to marry since we were both children. My mother, Lady Westwood, and Aunt Alicia have been great friends since their school days. But, of course, you wouldn't know anything about things like that. Tell me, do, what does it feel like having to earn your own living?'

'Very satisfying!' Kate snapped.

Veronica raised her pencilled eyebrows.

'Really? And you don't mind what you have to do so as to earn a crust?'

'I don't mind doing shorthand, typewriting and book-keeping, the things which I'm paid to do!'

'And the other? Although he must have been a very good-looking man in his youth, Uncle Peter is decidedly middle-aged and a trifle corpulent now.'

She got no further, for Kate was on her feet and openly glaring at the rich, spoiled beauty.

'I find your insinuations disgusting! I am not your Uncle Peter's mistress and never will be! In fact, I am dating Robbie Karran, Sir Peter's chauffeur, and very likely we will make a match of it!'

And then, without a by-your-leave, Kate swept out of the room, leaving Veronica looking after her, her pretty, little mouth hanging open.

166

9

What had she said! She'd more or less told the obnoxious Veronica that she was going to marry Robbie and even if it might well be the best thing for her to do, Kate was by no means sure that she would. Oh, her parents would be very pleased. Even if her father had been pleasantly surprised by Roger Grenville, Kate was sure that they would like to see her safely married to a steady, hard-working man of her own class.

And she had agreed to go to Robbie's parents' farm the next day. They would be setting out in the morning for Sunday dinner, served at lunch-time. Robbie had promised her a tour of the farm first.

Kate went downstairs, let herself out of the house and paced around the grounds like a caged lioness. She was getting herself in very deep. If she wasn't careful she would be in so deeply that she wouldn't be able to get out. The sound of the Bentley pulling into the drive broke into her troubled thoughts. Kate hid behind some hedging where she could see, but not be seen. She didn't want to be caught wandering around the grounds when she was supposed to be entertaining Veronica.

The car stopped outside the house and Robbie climbed out and was opening the passenger door. Roger Grenville, a scarf pulled up and hiding the injured side of his face, got out and then Sir Peter and Lady Alicia emerged from the back of the Bentley. Roger was home!

Although she didn't expect to, Kate slept soundly that night, although she did have a dream where Robbie became Roger and vice versa. But at least she slept and woke up feeling a bit better than she had done for the past few days.

Robbie had walked to the farm early

that morning and borrowed one of his father's two vans, as Sir Peter would be using the Bentley. It was almost a five-mile walk, but Robbie didn't mind. He was fit, and used to walking. He planned to enlist for the army any day now before he was actually called up. He could have avoided the call-up with his father being a farmer, but Robbie wasn't one to linger at home when his country needed him. The only thing he wanted to settle first was his engagement to Kate, and then they could marry during his first leave.

'Your parents know I'm coming,' Kate said.

'Yes, and they're delighted, just as I said they would be.'

So presumably they would welcome her. Kate smiled, but inside she was feeling nervous, her stomach churning as if butterflies were lodged there, and she wondered why. Robbie had three younger brothers and sisters and these Karrans were the first Kate met as they were waiting for the van to pull up in the farmyard. The youngest girl, four-year-old Mary, looked at Kate with wide eyes.

'Are you going to marry our Robbie and be my big sister?' she asked.

Kate was saved from answering by the elder girl, nine-year-old Lizzie.

'Oh, be quiet, young Mary. You don't go around asking adults questions like that!' she said.

'What are you going to do now, our Robbie?' one of the lads, a tousled-haired fellow, asked.

'I thought I'd give Kate a tour around the farm.'

'Aye, well, that's a good idea and all.'

'Watch out for Satan, though,' a tall, lanky fellow who couldn't have been much younger than Robbie said. 'He seems a bit cranky this morning.'

'He's safe in his field, is he? The one next to where the young bullocks and the cows are?'

'Yeah, the usual one.'

'Then you can have a look at him from a distance,' Robbie said, smiling at

Kate. 'He was a fine fellow in his day, but he's got arthritis now and it's making him grumpy. Really, Micky, I wonder why Pa doesn't get rid of him. He'd make good steak.'

The brother laughed as if Robbie had made a great joke but Kate found herself feeling decidedly out of place as Robbie led her over to a gate into one of the fields.

'That's him, that's the blighter! Got a look of Sir Peter, don't you think?'

Kate looked at the bull, a big black brute with a gold ring in his flaring nostrils and his feet stamping the ground. She shuddered. Robbie put his arm around her shoulders.

'I can see that you're not impressed! Come on into this field then.'

Kate reluctantly followed Robbie into the next field. Although she was fond of domestic animals, she wasn't too keen on cows. They were just too big, somehow. As soon as they entered the field, the cows began lumbering towards them. Kate couldn't help it but she found that she had drawn her breath in, and was backing away. Robbie laughed.

'They don't mean any harm, Kate. They're just curious, that's all. Stay still, and let them come and sniff you.'

But Kate was no longer listening to him, for rapidly overtaking the cows were a dozen or more lively bullocks and they were heading straight for her. Kate ran.

'Kate, no! That's the wrong thing to do!' Robbie cried. 'If you run, they'll think it's a game, and they'll chase you.'

But Kate was acting on pure impulse. She had to reach the gate, had to get out of the field before the bullock in front pounced on her and killed her. Robbie sighed. He couldn't stop the herd. He'd just have to try to hold back the bullocks who thought this was tremendous fun. He stood in their path, hoping to block Kate from their view and called to them in an authoritative voice to stop. Whether they would nor not, they never discovered, for Kate skidded on some mud and landed face down in a considerable mass of cow dung. The bullocks, with nothing to chase, quickly lost interest.

Robbie was soon at Kate's side and reached out a hand to help her up.

'Are you all right?' he asked, and then, when she clambered to her feet, obviously uninjured, he threw back his head and laughed. 'Good grief, Kate, but you look a right sight! There's muck all over your face and hair and . . . '

He got no further, because Kate, feeling a complete and utter fool, burst into tears. Kindly Mrs Karran appeared and took Kate up to the farmhouse bathroom and poured a bath for her.

'I'm sorry that there's no scented bath salts or nothing like that, but there's plenty of soap, so you'll be able to scrub yourself clean and wash your hair. I'd help you myself but I must see to dinner. I'll send young Lizzie up. She'll be only too pleased to give you a hand.'

'There's no need, thank you,' Kate

mumbled, wanting to be left alone.

Mrs Karran, seeing how upset the girl was, nodded. This one didn't seem the type for a farmer's wife and despite Robbie's flirtation with cars, both she and Burt Karran were hoping that he'd come back and take over the farm some day. But perhaps she'd toughen up, given time.

'All right, take your time, love. Just come down when you're ready.'

Kate mumbled her thanks and locked the bathroom door. Afterwards, Kate was aware that the day had been a complete and total disaster. Robbie was as quiet as was she and she felt that at least some of his siblings were laughing at her. Farmer Karran seemed a bit bewildered and although Mrs Karran was kind, Kate sensed that she wasn't what the farmer's wife would wish for as a daughter-in-law.

Kate was very glad when it was time to leave and although Mrs Karran said that she must come again, Kate felt that she was only being polite. She and

Robbie made a silent journey back to The Grange, and he excused himself immediately, saying that he would have to take his father's van back. Kate didn't attempt to detain him. After her humiliation, she just wanted to be on her own.

After the huge farmhouse meal, which, admittedly, Kate hadn't done justice to, she decided to go for a walk, and found herself following the cliffside path where she had gone riding with Roger Grenville. To her surprise, she came across Roger's horse, Nero, tethered to a tree, alerting Kate to the fact that he must be around somewhere. Then she saw him sitting as still as a statue, knees hunched up to his chest, staring out to sea.

He hadn't seen her and Kate wondered if she should retreat. She still had time, but her hesitation was her undoing, for taking a step forward and then one back, she stepped on a dry twig, which snapped with a crackling noise and made Roger turn round. Kate saw that there was a light dressing covering his left cheek.

'Kate,' he called, and then he was on his feet and walking towards her.

Kate stood as if she had been turned to stone.

'I want to apologise to you,' he said huskily. 'My behaviour when you came to see me at the hospital was unforgivable.'

Kate smiled.

'There's nothing to forgive,' she assured him. 'You'd had a dreadful experience and I should have warned you that I was coming.'

'No, you shouldn't, Kate. You wanted to give me a surprise and it would have been a lovely one if I hadn't been so steeped in self-pity! No, it was my fault entirely. I acted like a boor.'

'Don't worry about it, Roger. I've told you that it doesn't matter. I do understand.'

'Oh, Kate,' he murmured and then she was in his arms and his lips were against her hair.

Kate was just happy to be near him again, but as his mouth sought hers, realisation of what she was doing hit her just as if someone had thrown a glass of cold water into her face.

'No, no!' she murmured, her voice low, but she pulled out of his arms. 'It isn't right!'

He looked at her with eyes filled with pain.

'Because of Robbie Karran?'

'No,' Kate replied, 'because of Veronica Hill-Stevens.'

Then, because she didn't want to make a fool of herself twice in one day, she ran back down the path to the safety of her room at The Grange.

'Kate, wait!' he called desperately. 'Give me a chance to explain.'

But Kate knew there was no point. There was nothing he could say. Hadn't Veronica made it clear that she and Roger were intended for marriage practically from the cradle?

★　★　★

As he had hinted at previously, Robbie enlisted and would be going to Lancashire to begin his army training in just over a week's time.

'I was wondering, like, if you'd want to get engaged before I go,' he asked her, but he didn't meet her eyes and Kate had the distinct feeling that he was asking her because, good man that he undoubtedly was, he felt it could look to outsiders as if he'd just been stringing her along, but Kate still had the distinct impression that he didn't really want an engagement between them.

'It's lovely of you to ask me, Robbie, but can you really see me as a farmer's wife?'

He couldn't, and in his first unguarded look, it was quite obvious.

'That doesn't matter, Kate. I'm not a farmer, leastways, not for a while yet. Like I said, I love cars and tinkering about with them.'

'I know you do, Robbie,' Kate replied gently, 'but one day you'll go back to the farm.'

'Well, maybe I will, when Pa needs extra help. But that won't be for quite a while yet. By that time, well, you'll have changed, too, had plenty of time to learn how to be a farmer's wife.'

Kate looked at him sadly.

'Robbie, if I lived to be one hundred, I'd still never be any good on a farm. I'm frightened of farm animals.'

He took his cap off and scratched his head. He'd never heard anything like that before, but then, he'd never met anyone quite like Kate before.

'I tell you what, Robbie.' Kate smiled, seeing his total confusion. 'You go off and do your training, and then, when you come back on leave we can see how things are then.'

Robbie smiled.

'Yes, good idea! But you were always a clever one, Kate.'

Then his face clouded over.

'But what about the young master? What about Roger Grenville? You think I haven't got the brains to see that you two are interested in each other, but I have!'

Kate didn't argue.

'Roger and Miss Hill-Stevens will marry. She told me that they've been promised to one another since they were scarcely out of their prams.'

Robbie grinned, happy again.

'Oh, well, that's all right then!'

Perhaps that was so with Robbie, once he had gone to his Lancashire training centre, but it wasn't all right with Kate, who awaited the announcement of Roger's and Veronica's engagement on a daily basis. They seemed to spend enough time together and if Kate was to be totally honest with herself she would admit that she was consumed with jealousy. So much so that despite the fact that most of her secretarial work now took place at Sir Peter's factory, she knew that she couldn't go on living under the same roof as the young lovers.

Kate was still visiting Mrs Rogers regularly, and when the principal told her that Miss Sands, her assistant, was leaving any day, Kate almost begged her to let her have the position, which was a live-in one. Miss Sands had her own apartment above the school.

Mrs Rogers hesitated. She liked Kate very much and knew how skilled and conscientious she was. Although her exam results wouldn't be out for another week or so yet, Mrs Rogers had checked Kate's papers and was sure that she had passed, and probably with distinction.

'That would be a great help to me, Kate, dear. The only thing is that you don't have a teaching qualification. Still, that could quite easily be rectified. I could tutor you myself and I know that you'd pass easily.'

'Then it's all right? You'll give me Miss Sands' job?'

Mrs Rogers smiled.

'Yes, Kate, I will, although why you want it when you've got a good position with Sir Peter Grenville, I'll never know.'

Then a thought struck her. Sir Peter had a bad reputation where the ladies were concerned.

'He's not . . . er . . . he's not making overtures to you, is he, my dear?'

Kate hesitated. It would be so easy to agree but it wouldn't be fair. After that one incident, Sir Peter had been very circumspect towards her.

'No, it isn't that, Mrs Rogers, but I do want to leave The Grange.'

Mrs Rogers waited for Kate to say more, but when she didn't she didn't press her.

'Very well,' she said. 'How soon will you be able to start?'

Kate said she could start the following Monday.

Although she knew she wasn't really playing fair, Kate decided that it would be wiser to leave The Grange without telling anyone. She didn't want Roger to know and if she told Sir Peter then his son would surely get to know, too. She sneaked away on the Sunday evening when the family was at church and moved into the apartment recently vacated by Miss Sands.

The next couple of weeks passed very quickly because Kate was kept so busy. She didn't mind at all, as that way, she didn't have so much time to think about Roger.

As Mrs Rogers had suspected, Kate had passed her exams with distinction and with the principal's help, was diligently studying towards a teaching certificate. For a gardener's daughter, Kate had done very well and, in a way, she was quite proud of herself, although there was definitely something lacking in her life and she knew very well that that something was really a someone.

Shortly after classes had finished one pleasant summer's evening, Kate decided to sit outside for an hour or so in the small, private rear garden which came with the flat. She was just settling down with a novel when she realised that she wasn't alone.

'Bess, what on earth are you doing here?' she exclaimed and then saw that

Roger's black spaniel had come in through the garden gate, although for the life of her, Kate didn't remember leaving it ajar.

Then, as Roger appeared behind the dog, she realised that she hadn't. Face ashen, Kate spoke, her voice little more than a whisper.

'What are you doing here? How did you know I was here anyway?'

'I didn't until I approached Mrs Rogers to see if she knew anything. I'd already asked your parents, but they were as close as clams!'

'Yes, I told them to be!' Kate retorted defensively. 'But I'm surprised that Mrs Rogers told . . . '

Her voice trailed off. As she hadn't told the principal why she'd left The Grange, there was no reason at all why Mrs Rogers shouldn't have told Roger. Kate sighed.

'Why have you come, Roger? To torment me further by telling me when the wedding is?'

'If you're referring to Veronica, she's

not even on the island. She went back to London a few days ago.'

Kate was so surprised that she sat down, and Roger immediately took the opportunity of sitting down beside her on the garden seat, Bess standing in front of them, her little tail wagging fiercely as she wondered why they were ignoring her.

'But why?' Kate asked at length, then, her voice bitter, she added, 'I suppose there wasn't anything smart enough for her to buy for her wedding in the island shops!'

Roger tried to take one of her hands in his, but Kate pulled away from him. She'd noticed, however, that his left hand was no longer bandaged and that there was only a small, puckered scar on it. His face still bore the marks of the blaze in the barn, but the fierce colour had faded quite a bit.

'Veronica left because I told her that I didn't love her,' Roger said quietly. 'I also told my parents. My mother was a bit upset at first but my father, surprisingly, actually laughed! He said that he'd been expecting something of the sort, and he couldn't really find it in his heart to blame me, because he wasn't that struck on Veronica either!'

Kate's eyes were very wide and bright as she responded, her voice little more than a whisper, so that Roger had to lean forward in order to hear her.

'But why? Why did you do that?'

'I was just telling the truth. I don't love Veronica and never could, as my affections are most definitely deeply entrenched elsewhere!' He smiled. 'Kate, I'd have been here as soon as she left, only there was something which I had to do first. I had to find out that I would be accepted for the Services, that my burns hadn't incapacitated me to an extent where I wouldn't be accepted.'

Kate smiled back at him.

'From what I can see, your injuries seem to be healing up very well.'

'They are, and I've got a clean bill of health. I'm in, Kate, and I'm leaving to do my pilot training later this month.'

So she would lose him again, just when she was beginning to think that they might have a future together after all. Kate sighed. She supposed that she shouldn't really be too surprised. She couldn't look at him, though. She was afraid that he would see the pain mirrored in her eyes. Kate bent her head and tickled Bess behind her long, velvety ears.

'I'm very happy for you.'

He could hardly hear her, and she seemed to be addressing the dog rather than him! Roger was suddenly very ill at ease. Kate had left The Grange and made her own life, her own career. She was a talented young woman and he was going to ask her to bury her talent and come away with him. He took a deep breath.

'Kate, do you still care, about me, I mean?' he said.

He was sounding like a stammering schoolboy, Roger thought, consumed by self-disgust. And before Kate had time to reply, he hurried on.

'Because I'd like you to marry me and come with me to the base. They've got married quarters there, you know. And then when I'm sent overseas, you can come back to the island and continue with your teacher training and . . . '

He stopped. He sounded as if he was organising Kate's whole life for her!

'I'm sorry,' he said. 'I didn't mean to sound as if I'm taking over. It's just that I want this so very much!'

He looked at Kate with eyes filled with love and tenderness. Still she said nothing, and Roger, his nerves feeling as tight as violin strings, spoke again.

'Say something, please!'

Kate laughed and Roger looked bewildered.

'You silly goose, of course I'll marry you!'

'Oh, Kate!'

Roger immediately took her into his arms and covered her face with kisses, with Bess yapping excitedly as she danced around their feet.

SUMMER IN HANOVER SQUARE

Charlotte Grey

The impoverished Margaret Lambart is suddenly flung into all the glitter of the Season in Regency London. Suspected by her godmother's nephew, the influential Marquis St. George, of being merely a common adventuress, she has, nevertheless, a brilliant success, and attracts the attentions of the young Duke of Oxford. However, when the Marquis discovers that Margaret is far from wanting a husband he finds he has to revise his estimate of her true worth.

CONFLICT OF HEARTS

Gillian Kaye

Somerset, at the end of World War I: Daniel Holley, unhappily married to an ailing wife and father of four grown-up children, is attracted to beautiful schoolteacher Harriet Bray, but he knows his love is hopeless. Daniel's only daughter, Amy, who dreams of becoming a milliner and is caught up in her love for young bank clerk John Tottle, looks on as the drama of Daniel and Harriet's fate and happiness gradually unfolds.

THE SOLDIER'S WOMAN

Freda M. Long

When Lieutenant Alain d'Albert was deserted by his girlfriend, a replacement was at hand in the shape of Christina Calvi, whose yearning for respectability through marriage did not quite coincide with her profession as a soldier's woman. Christina's obsessive love for Alain was not returned. The handsome hussar married an heiress and banished the soldier's woman from his life. But Christina was unswerving in the pursuit of her dream and Alain found his resistance weakening . . .

THE TENDER DECEPTION

Laura Rose

When Sophia Barton was taken from Curton Workhouse to be a scullery-maid at Perriman Court, her future looked bleak. Was it really an act of Providence that persuaded Lady Perriman to adopt her as her ward? Sophia was brought up together with the Perriman children, and before sailing with his regiment for India, George, the heir to the title, declared his love. But tragedy hit the family and Sophia found herself caught up in a web of mystery and intrigue.